Sarah's Prayer

Bobbie Joe Yates

Published by Trellis Publishing, 2021.

SARAH'S PRAYER

First edition. July 16, 2021.

ISBN: 979-8224093083

Written by Bobbie Joe Yates.

SARAH'S PRAYER

BOBBI JOE YATES

Chapter One

Pastor Michael seemed more agitated this session, Sarah noticed, making sure to write that down in her notepad. Not that that was something she would ever use against him, but it was useful information in gaining insight into his psyche. He'd been coming to her for marriage counseling for three months now, and she still didn't really know what the deeper issue interrupting his marriage was.

"There are sometimes when I just have to see you without Eileen," Michael said suddenly, spinning to face her and pinning her with what Sarah called his Church Gaze: stern eyes that could pierce her soul if they chose to. "I know you know her, probably better than I do, since you both seem to understand one another and I don't know if I've ever understood her. But Sarah, you don't know what it's like, living with her, doing everything with her."

Sarah nodded sagely. "You feel you've grown together too much," she said.

Michael laughed bitterly. "Quite the opposite," he said.

Sarah frowned. "You feel that she is growing away from the church and leaving you behind?" she asked.

Michael shook his head. "No, it's nothing like that," he said, sounding tormented. "Instead, I know I should be devoting my life towards God and towards the church. But instead, I–" He broke off, looking guilty.

"You...?" Sarah prodded questioningly. Michael was one of her more frustrating clients since he had a tendency to frequently break off in the middle of a thought. She was starting to realize he would break off whenever he felt something he was about to say might be blasphemous, but she was also starting to realize that those supposedly blasphemous things that he was about to say were the key to solving this whole thing. It kept her on the edge of her seat each time, waiting for the one time when he managed to finish a thought without the fear of God stopping him.

Michael stared at her for a long moment, and Sarah thought with a sinking heart that he wasn't going to finish the thought. But then, he wet his lips and cleared his throat a little. "I find that I'm...drawn to someone else," he admitted.

Sarah blinked at him, surprised to get that truth from him. Of course, it didn't mean there was nothing wrong with his marriage since there had to be something driving this principled, moral man towards another woman, but if the main reason he and Eileen were coming to marriage counseling was because Michael fancied himself in love with another woman, it certainly changed things. She doubted he would ever act on those feelings, for one thing, and for another, that meant this was probably just a bit of a midlife crisis on his part—it wasn't that he was dissatisfied with his current situation, he just thought he should make a bit of a change. She just had to make him see that he could do that from inside of the relationship.

"Eileen knows you're drawn to someone else?" Sarah asked slowly.

Michael sighed and slumped down on one of the sofas, his long legs akimbo. "I don't know," he answered honestly. "This other woman, she's not the reason we first started coming here. But she's becoming...more of the reason we're still coming here."

"Has Eileen seen you interact with this other woman?"

Michael exhaled noisily. "Yes, she has. The woman is a member of our parish, and we talk often—even outside of church functions. I do my best not to let things escalate beyond talking—absolutely no touching or anything like that. As much as I long to..."

Sarah frowned at him. "Well, that's good. That shows a reluctance to give up on what you have with Eileen." She paused, trying to think of a delicate way to phrase what she wanted to say next. "And what does, uh, God have to say about...all of this?" Well, so much for delicacy.

Michael dropped his head into his hands. "I'm too close to the matter," he told her, his voice raw with emotion. "I'm afraid I'm not able to objectively interpret the will of God on this matter."

Sarah stared at him for a moment, shock written on her face. That had to be tormenting him, after all his years of service to the church and to God. She was struck with the sudden desire to move to the couch next to him and lay a hand on his shoulder.

When she did so, Michael blinked over at her, looking momentarily not like the stern pastor she'd come to know but rather like a lost, lonely, rather ordinary man. Up close like this, she could see the bags beneath his eyes, hinting at fitful nights of sleep.

She lightly squeezed his shoulder.

Michael brought his hand slowly up to cover hers, but then he yanked away as though he'd been burnt, standing abruptly and looking at his watch. "I'm afraid I have to go," he said, nearly tripping over himself in his haste.

"Michael," Sarah said, surprised at how firm her voice was. Michael paused at the door and half-turned back towards her. "Running away from your feelings isn't going to get you anywhere," she scolded.

The pastor seemed to deflate a little. "I don't want to do something I'll regret," he said hoarsely. "I think that Eileen and I need to stop seeing you. It's been a pleasure—believe me, it has—but I can't..."

Sarah frowned and took a couple steps towards him, holding out her hand imploringly. "Wait a minute, Michael," she said quietly. "Come on, let's sit down on the couch and talk for a minute. Explain to me what the problem is."

Michael looked like he was about ready to tear his hair out. "It's you, don't you get it?" the man said, sounding pained. "Ever since Eileen and I started coming here, I've become more and more...smitten by you." He blushed and looked away from her.

Sarah stared at him for a long moment, totally lost for words. After all these months of trying to get truth out of him, she wanted, on one hand, to rejoice at how open he was finally being with her. But on the other hand, she couldn't deny the awkward position that he was putting her in. There had to be something in her contract against her taking advantage of people who came to her for counseling. And even if there wasn't, there had to be something morally wrong with it.

But she was fixated with the way that for the first time, she could see what a handsome man the pastor was. His dark hair fell in waves that didn't quite reach his eyes, which stood out from his chiseled cheekbones as though the Greeks had sculpted him from a block of pristine marble. When he blinked those clear blue eyes...

She swallowed hard.

"I know," Michael sighed, looking away from her. "You haven't even finalized your divorce yet. And I haven't even asked for a divorce from Eileen yet, even though I know in my heart of hearts that this clearly isn't working. I don't know where it went wrong, even. She's been the perfect wife for me, and yet I... It started so small. We thought we could fix it. But the more we try to fix it, the more I become convinced that it's not something we could fix. And it's not just that I'm finding myself more attracted to you than I ever was to her. It's just..." He trailed off, shaking his head. "I try to tell myself that it's a test from God, but that no longer comforts me like it used to."

Sarah tried desperately to process his words, to formulate some sort of response. She thought for a minute about David, about everything that she'd had in the life that she'd built with him. About the day that David had told her that he wanted a divorce. The trouble was, everything that she felt for David ground to a halt when she thought of those divorce papers, the copy of which she kept buried in her sock drawer, a quiet reminder of her failure.

"I don't make a good wife," she blurted suddenly, surprised to feel the tears in her eyes.

For a moment, Michael looked torn, as though he wanted desperately to come to her side, to comfort her. But there was something there that was holding him back, just as she might expect. He stumbled a couple steps back, reaching his hand out to grasp the doorknob. "Sarah," he said, voice sounding absolutely wrecked with his feelings. "Sarah, I have to go." And without another word, he fled from her office.

Sarah sank down on one of the plush couches and curled into herself, trying her best not to sob.

Chapter Two

The rest of the day passed in a bit of a blur for Sarah. She had a couple other appointments, but fortunately, there was nothing too tricky that she had to deal with: she didn't know that she would have been able to figure out the intricacies that plagued some of her clients. Indeed, she could hardly figure out the questions that she meant to ask her less-tricky clients.

"Sarah, are you feeling okay?" Carrie asked her in her final session of the day.

Sarah blinked over at the woman, trying desperately to remember what the woman's husband had just been speaking about. But she couldn't seem to remember. She shook her head slowly. "I'm afraid I need to end this session early," she said quietly. "I'm sorry, I just– I'm not feeling so good tonight."

Carrie smiled gently at her, while George looked like he wanted to roll his eyes but didn't dare to. They both politely got up to leave, making her promise that she would go home and sleep with her unexpected free time.

Instead, Sarah lay back on one of the couches and closed her eyes, unable to face the whitewashed ceiling and sterile-but-cozy environment that she and David had designed in that office.

She lay there for a long time, but she was no closer to mental resolution by the time she finally sat up. She had to go home. She would need to pick up dinner on the way home, because there was nothing left in the house that she could make into any sort of respectable dinner. And then she would need to sort through her notes from the day and get everything in order for the next day. Maybe she would watch something stupid on television for the end of the night. Then she would set her alarm and fall into her lonely, cold bed. The next morning, she would wake up early and start it all over again.

That's what her life had become, After David: a series of tasks that she knew she needed to complete. And she didn't want to say that she felt any sort of pride with each new day that she managed to tick her way through, but...well, it was kind of true that she did. And, hey, whatever got you out of bed in the morning, right?

When she got home to a house where all the lights were on, her first instinct was to blink her eyes and look around, as though ten years after moving to this house, she might have accidentally parked in one of her neighbor's driveways. But no, this was definitely 116 Fulker's Drive—she could see the house number clearly in the beam of her headlights.

For a moment, she thought she might have left the house lights all on that morning. But while she might have turned on the kitchen light in the early light of the day, there was no way she would have ever needed the light in the living room. There had to be someone else in there.

She sat staring at the house for a long time, her fingers white on the leather steering wheel. It was possible that someone had broken in. But what would they have taken from her, anyways? She didn't have much, since they'd started the process of the divorce. David had always bought most of their things, and she hadn't felt much like fighting him when he'd claimed it all back in the divorce. Her lawyer had tried to argue, back when this had first started, but when Sarah had refused to go along with it, her lawyer had got sick of it and just let her dictate their course of action. There were very few things that held meaning to her there in the house, and they weren't the sorts of things that would attract the eye of a thief.

She didn't call the police. Instead, after a long moment, she switched off her headlights and stepped out of the car, heading slowly into the house.

When she saw David sitting there on the couch, her first thought was that she must be more tired than she'd thought she was. She rubbed tiredly at her eyes, but when she opened them again, he was still there staring back at her. And when he moved, well. That was when she really started to believe that he was truly there. No matter how she'd memorized his movements over the years, she was sure a figment of her imagination wouldn't achieve the level of grace that he did.

"What are you doing here?" she asked hoarsely.

David paused, looking at her. "You look like hell," he told her, but his words were gentle, as though it were five years ago and he wanted to pull her into his arms and help her relax after a long day.

Sarah fought back a wave of tears. "I can't deal with you here tonight," she told him. "I can't…" She was in tears before she really realized it, all the stress of the meeting with Michael catching up to her. She didn't know what she wanted with her future, but it seemed like the universe itself was pressuring her to decide. And how was she to make that choice?

"Oh Sarah," David breathed, breaching the distance between the two of them and pulling the woman into his arms. "Oh Sarah."

They were both silent for a long time, both swaying slightly to the sound of some unheard song.

It was Sarah who finally pulled away. "I can't–" she started.

"Shh," David said, even going so far as to place a finger over her lips. He squeezed his eyes shut briefly, the most emotion Sarah had seen out of him in months—if not years. "Sarah, I don't want to go through on the divorce," he said.

Sarah stared at him and then, despite herself, started to laugh. "David, we've been processing this divorce for *months* now," she reminded him. She waved her hand around the half-barren house.

"You've taken all your things from here. You've moved into the house on Somerset Street. And–"

Again, David placed the finger over her lips. "Sarah," he said, his voice sounding hurt, "just listen to me for a minute, would you? Please."

Sarah shook her head, though. "Oh no," she said, drawing back away. "Oh no. No, you don't get to ask that, not now. Not when you wouldn't tell me why you were divorcing me until you had served me the papers. Not when–"

David shook his head. "I've done a lot of thinking, Sarah," he said, sounding hurt. "Sarah, you don't know how it's felt like, divorcing you. When all I really wanted was to talk things over with you. But it wasn't like we could go to a marriage counselor. You would have picked them apart, point by point. Everything would have been on your terms. I didn't know how to... I just didn't know what I was doing. I'm sorry."

Sarah shook her head again. "We can't do this," she whispered.

For the first time, it was David pulling away. "Is there someone else?" he asked.

Sarah was silent for a long time. They stared at one another. Sarah could remember falling in love with David. He had been so handsome—*was* so handsome, although in an entirely different sense from Michael. Where Michael had that classical, chiseled handsomeness, David's looks could only be described as *pretty*—but it was a prettiness that transcended genders. It was there in his smooth, thin fingers—in the graceful way that he moved—in the angular features of his face.

And there had been the care that he'd shown for her. And his sense of humor. It was his personality, above everything, that she'd fallen for.

But she could remember the day he'd asked for a divorce, clearer than any other day in her life. She could have told you what both of them were wearing, where they were, what the very *air* around them smelled like. She could have told you the song that was playing out the doors of the nearby shop.

She couldn't have told you how it felt, having her heart broken like that. That was the one thing that she knew she would never have the words for.

"There might be someone else," she finally admitted, unable to meet his eyes. She swallowed hard.

David exhaled noisily through his nose. "I thought there might be," he finally said. He laughed a little. "I guess I had my epiphany moment too late, hmm?"

Sarah didn't know how to answer that. "I didn't say that there *was* someone," she finally pointed out, because by now, it was a conditioned response to be truthful to him. "I admitted that there *might* be someone." She ducked her head, wishing almost that she hadn't told him that. That was as good as challenging him to win her back, something that she didn't want.

David had been the one to ask her out. He'd been the one to ask her to move in with him. He'd been the one to ask her to meet his family. And he'd been the one to ask her to marry him. Everything about their relationship had been initiated by him; for once, she kind of wanted to make her own decisions.

What if she wanted to try this thing with Michael?

The thought came unbidden, and it caused her to blush a little. She picked at the edge of her sleeve as though it were the most fascinating thing in the world. "David, I'm going to need you to leave now," she said in a voice that she hardly recognized as hers.

"I want to take you out," he said quietly. He didn't move from his spot, and he held up his hands placatingly.

Sarah stared at him. But she couldn't forget all the memories they had made together. "When?" she finally asked, her voice hardly audible.

Chapter Three

The one thing she could be happy for, she reflected, was that David wasn't stupid enough to bring her back to the place that they'd had their first date. As much as she loved that place, there were too many memories attached to it, and she knew it would hurt to be back there, with their relationship in its current state. Instead, he had selected a Moroccan restaurant that they had never eaten at before. Sarah appreciated the choice, especially because she knew he didn't like Moroccan food that much. He was making this about her.

They were both clearly nervous, she reflected, as he rushed around to open her door for her.

She blushed and looked up at him through her lashes as she arranged her shawl around her. "David, you don't need to impress me," she said quietly. "Remember, you already got me to marry you once." It wasn't meant as a dig; instead, it was more a statement of fact. But she could see the way he winced.

"Sarah, I want you to forget about that tonight," he said quietly. "I want you to focus on now, on tonight. I want to–"

Sarah burst out laughing, unable to help herself. Not only was that unhealthy, but– "That's impossible," she told him. "Although if what you're trying to tell me is that you can forget the fact that we were once married, well. I guess I can see why–"

"That's not it," David interrupted. He scrubbed a hand over his face, looking momentarily exhausted. "Sarah, that's not it at all. You know that. You know I could never forget what it was like to be married to you." He smiled a little at her. "We were such good friends, weren't we?"

Sarah sighed and looked away. "David," she said warningly.

"Okay," David said, catching her arm and tugging her towards the doorway of the restaurant. "Let's forget about that—about all of that. For tonight, for just one night, I want to start anew. If we can. I think we can." He paused, eyes hesitantly searching her face. "I want to act like this is our first date, like we're going into this with no baggage behind us," he told her. "Of course we were married. Of course we know one another better than most people do, first date or fiftieth date. But I want to pretend like—"

"I don't know if I can do that," Sarah said, before he could go any further. She shook her head. "Even being here, with all of our baggage—that's enough for me to sort through."

David was silent for a moment. He lightly brushed a lock of hair behind Sarah's ear. "I always loved how blunt you were," he said.

Sarah sighed and pushed him away a little. "We can love however many small parts of the other person's personality," she said. "But in the long run, that doesn't mean we're going to be okay, married to one another."

David nodded sagely. "But Sarah, what else are you going to look for?" he asked.

Sarah frowned, thinking about Michael even though she knew she should be focusing her thought on this current date. Somehow, though, she knew that Michael would have understood this better than anyone else—the idea of being married to someone, loving someone so much, and then having to come to the realization that maybe you were never meant to be together.

She would have expected Michael to have that same understanding as her, but then again, she had expected Michael to remain happily married to her for the rest of their lives.

She followed him into the restaurant.

They were mostly silent while they looked over the menu and placed their orders. When the waitress had walked away, Sarah laughed a little nervously, folding her hands on the table. "I don't really know what to say," she admitted. "This has all just kind of been...out of the blue."

David sighed and reached over, taking her hands in his. "I've really missed you lately," he said quietly. "I've missed *us*. And I've been trying to work on...well, everything. Myself. I'd like for you to see me as I am now. I'm happier."

Sarah shook her head and pulled her hands away. "You can't just..." She shook her head again.

"Sarah, we needed to take a break, you know that as well as I do," David insisted. "We were stagnating. We were doing the same things over and over and over again, and having the same fights over and over and over again. There's only so much of that that a relationship can take. We needed to find ourselves again as separate entities so that we could—"

"I don't," Sarah interrupted.

"You don't what?" David asked, faltering a little.

"I don't know that we needed a break," Sarah said. Her hands spasmed, momentarily clenching into fists. "That's the thing. This whole divorce thing...that was your idea. I didn't even realize there was a problem, I didn't even realize we were...stagnating, if that's what you think we were doing. You didn't even give me a chance to fix things, a chance to work through things. You just told me it was over and that there was nothing else I could do."

They were both silent for a moment.

"It was hard for me as well," David said quietly. "Don't forget that. Don't think I didn't think it through, torment myself with the thought of it day after day for months."

"Is that supposed to make me feel better about it?" Sarah snapped. "The fact remains—I trusted you. You were my best friend, you were my everything. And then suddenly you were just...gone. Without even a concrete reason. Do you know how long it took me to put myself back together?"

"But that's it, Sarah, that's exactly what we needed," David pleaded. "That's exactly what I'm saying. We've both worked on ourselves, found ourselves as individual entities again, and—"

Sarah stood abruptly. "I don't know what I expected from tonight, but I don't think I can do this. It's too painful, David." She took a deep breath. "I still want that divorce, even if you don't."

David caught her wrist with one hand, pinching the bridge of his nose with the other hand. "Wait, Sarah. Can you just sit down, please? Can we talk about this? I want to know what you've been up to lately, what–"

Sarah pulled her arm away. "I wanted to talk," she said hoarsely. "I wanted to talk, back when you wanted to get a divorce. And you wouldn't let me. I don't want to talk anymore. I want to put you in the past and move on with my life. It's taken me ages to get to this point, and I don't want to undo all the work that I've done. So I'm going to leave."

"You don't want to get hurt again," David said. "That's what it really comes down to, isn't it?"

Sarah paused for a moment, searching inside herself for the answer to that question. "It's not that I don't want to get hurt again," she said, glancing back at the man. "I'm sure I'll open up to someone else, when the time is right and I'm ready for it. But I don't want to get hurt by *you* again—no."

With that, she turned and strode out of the restaurant.

Chapter Four

That night, Sarah lay there in bed thinking about her two options. On the one hand, of course, there was David. She'd married the man for a reason. He was beautiful, he was kind, and she'd always pictured a future with him. She'd thought that one day, they would have children, that they would...

But she couldn't ignore the ways that they'd grown apart from one another. And she couldn't forget that hopeless feeling that she'd had when he'd asked her for a divorce, totally blindsiding her with his conviction that they were never meant for one another, despite the harmonious life they'd built with one another.

On the other hand, there was Michael. Michael was a good man, and he seemed to understand her better than she could ever have expected. He was charismatic and witty, and he always kept up a good conversation. He was having trouble in his own marriage, so he would understand where she was coming from. And for whatever reason, he had said that he liked her.

Without conscious direction from her mind, she found her right hand grasped around the phone, her left fingers punching out Michael's phone number, which she hadn't even realized she had memorized.

No one picked up, which wasn't too surprising since it was—she squinted at the clock—three in the morning. She blushed and dropped the phone back onto her nightstand. Anyway, it was probably for the best: what the hell did she think she was going to say to him?

The thing was, though, she wanted to tell him about David coming back, about him asking her to not go through with the divorce after all. She wanted to talk to Michael, to sort through all her complicated feelings about this situation. To tell him that in the end, Michael himself was one of the major obstacles keeping her from happily going back to David and the life she had previously led.

Maybe they had been stagnating. The thought of returning to the same life that she'd been living for the better part of twenty years made her frown. She didn't think things would be easy with Michael—he would need to go through with a divorce, and who knew what the parish would think about that. And she did like Eileen; she didn't want to hurt the woman. And then there were all of the challenges of a new relationship: getting to know the other person, learning to compromise with them, getting used to their unique quirks... There was a possibility that she would choose Michael over David, only to have both of those relationships fall through.

But then she would find someone else. Sarah was actually surprised at how firmly her mind supplied that thought. When David had first left her, she'd thought she would be alone forever.

She smiled a little, the marriage counselor part of herself recognizing what a big step this was for her. Finally, it seemed like her mind calmed a little, and she drifted off to sleep.

In the morning, it was back to chaos in her mind, but she managed to push through it to do her work as usual. At least until Michael appeared in her doorway, twisting his hands together.

"Are you busy?" the man asked.

Sarah barely spared a glance for the pile of paperwork that she was sorting through. "What's wrong?" she asked.

Michael took a couple hesitant steps into the room. "I wanted to let you know that..." He trailed off, looking uncertain. Then, he took a deep breath. "I wanted to let you know that I filed for a divorce from Eileen," he told her. He took another couple steps and sat rigidly on the edge of one of the couches. "She's a very good woman, but I don't know...how to do right by her anymore. She deserves better than me."

"That's a dangerous way to think," Sarah said clinically, looking down at the pen she had been using. "You need to accept your flaws, and you need to allow the other person to accept them as well. If Eileen is willing to–"

"Stop," Michael interrupted. When Sarah looked up at him, surprise on her face, he shook his head, a small smile on his lips. "This isn't a session," he told her. "This is two...friends...having a conversation. I don't need you to psychoanalyze everything. In fact, I'd prefer that you didn't."

Sarah blinked at him. "Friends?" she asked.

Michael looked momentarily uncertain. "Well, I hoped so, anyway. I mean, I won't be your client anymore since you kind of have to have a marriage in order to need marriage counseling, but maybe I could take you out for coffee sometime."

Sarah stared at him for a long moment and then smiled hesitantly. "I'd like that," she said quietly. She picked up her pen, twirling it between her fingers. "We should wait until after your divorce is finalized," she said, carefully not looking at the man. "You have…a lot of influence around town. You wouldn't want them to think…"

"You're right," Michael said, standing abruptly. "You're very right." He smiled at her and gave an aborted wave. Sarah couldn't help but smile at the way the stern, aloof pastor had suddenly been stripped away and replaced by this nervous, entirely-human man. "I'll see you in a few months, then, Sarah. Take care of yourself."

Chapter Five

Sarah tugged nervously at her sleeves while she waiting for Michael to reach her. It seemed like every member of the congregation wanted to thank him for that morning's sermon—which admittedly had been one of the most moving ones that Sarah had ever heard, but still. She felt like she was practically vibrating out of her skin, waiting anxiously for him.

The last person in the line of people waiting to speak to the man was Eileen, Sarah was surprised to see. Of course, she'd seen the woman there in the church, but she hadn't expected her to approach Michael. It had taken Sarah much longer before she'd worked up the courage to put aside her feelings of hurt and speak to David again.

Eileen took Michael's hands in hers, leaning in close and murmuring something. Whatever it was that she had said, Michael laughed at it, and Sarah had to quash an irrational flare of jealousy and uncertainty. They both had pasts; that was something that was unavoidable. She couldn't feel jealous every time Michael and Eileen interacted with one another, especially not when they were still living in the same small town and still going to the same church. She wouldn't have wanted Michael to feel jealous about her history with David either. It was something that was in the past, and it would stay there.

Besides, Michael had chosen to end his marriage with the woman. Sarah knew she had to trust in that.

Eileen finally broke away from Michael and smiled knowingly over her shoulder at Sarah. Sarah blinked at her and turned questioning eyes to Michael, who gave a little shrug as he made his way over to her. It made sense that he had told her, she supposed, when she really thought about it. In a town like theirs, she was likely to find out anyway. Better that she hear about it from Michael instead of someone else.

Michael finally reached her and held out his arm to her. "Shall we?" he asked in his deep voice.

Sarah smiled hesitantly up at him. "Let's," she agreed, slipping her hand into the inside of the man's elbow. "That really was a great sermon, you know," she said as they walked out of the churchyard. "Everything about forgiveness and... Well, a lot of it really hit home to me."

"I should hope so," Michael said, the corners of his lips quirking upwards. "I wrote most of that sermon while Eileen and I were coming to you for marriage counseling. A lot of the themes were the themes that we covered during our sessions. And I finished the sermon last week, after the divorce was finalized. I'm sure you, as a divorcee yourself, understood that sermon better than almost everyone else in town."

Sarah was silent for a long moment. "Do you regret it?" she asked.

Michael paused and drew Sarah around to face him. "Not one bit," he said seriously, his piercing gaze glued firmly on her. "Sarah, Eileen and I had something very special—as, I imagine, you and David did. But..." He reached out and tucked a lock of hair gently behind Sarah's ear. "You don't know how much I want to kiss you right now," he said in an undertone. "But I don't think that would be appropriate, given how recent my divorce was."

Sarah burst out laughing. "You sound like a teenager," she said. "Can't keep your hands off me?"

Michael smiled at her. "Well, you are gorgeous, I hope you realize." He shook his head and turned them so that they were walking again. "But for now, let's get to know one another better. Tell me about yourself, Ms. Sarah Walker."

Sarah shook her head, bumping her shoulder against his. "That's a pretty broad question," she said. "I'm not sure where to begin."

"Let's start with yesterday," Michael said, laughing a little. "What did you do yesterday? But before you answer, just know that I've set myself a goal: one day, I want to know everything about you. So you'd better be ready to tell me *all* about yourself. It just doesn't have to all be now."

Sarah laughed as well. "Okay," she said. "Sounds like a plan."

She smiled shyly at the man as he held the door open for her and ushered her into the coffee shop. For the first time since her divorce, she could feel hope blooming in her chest.

BRENDA'S REGRETS

SARAH THORNE

Brenda stared at the dark sidewalk while she waited for her taxi outside of the airport. The day had just begun to warm up and she regretted wearing so many layers of clothing. She had taken the first flight out of the city at the break of dawn so it had been cold when she left, but now her double sweaters were unnecessary in the blazing sun. Just as she began contemplating to go back inside to change her outfit in the women's restroom, she spotted the cab that was to take her back to her hometown. She recognized the dusty, bright yellow cab with the large white decal text reading *Mayville Cab Services* across the back windshield. Usually, cab companies declined their services to the people leaving or entering the town because it was so remote. Brenda's hometown—Mayville—had no other choice but to start their own cab service.

When the driver pulled up, he walked over to Brenda and put her suitcase and duffel bags in the trunk. The young man asked her if she was sure Mayville was her destination just to make sure because it was rare for people to need the cab service. She nodded as he opened the cab door for her. Mayville was still about two hours from the airport so she had plenty of time to nap in the spacious backseat of the cab but she was unable to put herself to sleep. She wondered if all of the things and people she had left behind 4 years ago were still there. She had fallen out with almost everybody after she had left, with the exception of her parents. They still kept in touch with her while she was away at college and would occasionally stop by for short visits. After she had moved to the city, little by little, she lost contact with everybody from Mayville. It didn't seem like such a big deal to her at the time but that all changed when she realized she had made a mistake by ever abandoning her home.

The further the cab drove away from the airport, the less buildings they passed. There were less cars, less people and less businesses. Eventually they were on a road surrounded by grass and fields with not even a cow in sight. Brenda used to hate the sense of living in the middle of nowhere, being unknown to the rest of the world. She was so eager to escape to the big city before she was even graduated from high school. She had taken this simple life for granted and was truly afraid that nobody would welcome her back to it. Brenda was so deep in thought about her worries that she had not noticed the driver looking at her through the rear-view mirror.

"Brenda? Brenda Jones?" he called out in a raspy voice.

"Yes, I'm Brenda Jones. Do we know each other?" she replied. The man seemed completely unfamiliar to her.

"It's me, Tom Foster, from the peach farm. My father would always give you guys our best peaches for your mother's peach cobbler. Your parents are Sandra and Mike, right?"

"Oh my god," Sandra exclaimed, "Little Tommy? Look at you! You're all grown up now! The last time I saw you, you were still picking on girls and pranking the townspeople. How are your parents?"

"Oh, they're great. Still running their peach farm and everything. I'm helping Eddie with his cab service—remember him?"

"I do. I expected to see him driving this old thing. Is he alright?"

"Yeah, he's doin' alright but he's got arthritis on his knees and can't stand driving for too long."

"Oh, that's too bad."

"Are you still playing basketball? Last I heard, you were headed to the NCAA Championship."

"You mean like on a team? No, I haven't played basketball since I graduated. I finally made it to the championship during my senior year of college and we ended up losing."

"I'm sorry to hear that. I mean, at least you experienced something like that. Most kids from Mayville never even step out of the town's borders."

"You know, Tom, you are so right. I'm not even bitter about it. I am really excited to be back in town, though; the city doesn't compare to the charm Mayville has."

They passed by a large field of yellow, red and purple tulips that gently swayed in the soft breeze. The view inspired her to buy flowers for her mother so she asked Tom if they could stop by the town superstore, Super Savers, before he dropped her off at home. Her mother loved receiving flowers and it had been a while since Brenda gifted her with some. Tim and Brenda talked throughout the remainder of the ride. Tim was very intrigued by the way things were in the city and had many questions for her until finally, they arrived at the store.

Brenda had planned to quickly run into the store for her mother's flowers and go on her way so Tim decided to wait for her in the cab. Even though Brenda knew where the flowers were, she perused through the aisles feeling completely nostalgic about her memories there. Brenda remembered shopping trips with her parents and sister since her days as a child. She stopped in front of a shelf displaying mugs with cute animal characters on it and grabbed a brown mug that was supposed to resemble a puppy. The curled up tail was the handle of the mug and it had cute facial features and ears painted on it. Brenda smiled at the funny mug while she held it in her hands. She stretched out her arm to put the mug back on the shelf when suddenly, a little boy wearing a red t-shirt and jeans ran past her. He bumped right into her arm and caused her to drop the mug, breaking it.

"Hey!" Brenda cried in astonishment and looked as the boy ran away. He didn't even stop. A chubby cashier heard the commotion and headed towards Brenda. He began picking up the pieces of broken ceramic.

"That mug costs five ninety-nine. You'll have to pay for it at the cash register," the cashier said matter-of-factly.

"I'm not paying for that! That little boy was running around in the store so his parents should pay for the damaged mug," Brenda said displeased.

"Ma'am, you were the one holding the mug. You shouldn't have dropped it," the cashier replied, still speaking in a monotone voice.

"That's so unfair! You don't really expect me to pay for that, do you? His parents should have been taking care of him."

"I don't work here to judge other people's parenting, ma'am. You dropped the mug, you have to pay for it."

"I would like to speak to your manager right now," Brenda said.

"Okay," the cashier replied, rolling his eyes, "let me go get him."

Brenda waited by the mug display and browsed the shelf, scoffing at the event that had occurred. She muttered, "So ridiculous. That boy ran into my arm and *I* have to pay for it. Oh, please!" Footsteps falling on the tile prompted her to look up towards whoever was coming to her. It was the cashier with the manager besides him and apparently, the little boy accompanied them as well. The manager looked very familiar to Brenda. The closer he got, the more certain she was about who it was. Then, he was right in front of her. She stood there, mouth agape. Brenda's heart beat so hard it could have ripped right through her chest. Her stomach was in a knot and she could already feel the beads of sweat forming on her forehead.

"What is the problem?" the manager asked her. He looked at her with a frowning expression. Brenda stood there wide-eyed and speechless. When the cashier felt the awkward atmosphere he slowly explained the situation to the manager who didn't take his eyes off of Brenda's for a second. The manager grabbed the little boy's hand and sternly said, "Donnie, how many times do I have to remind you not to run inside the store? This is already the second time you break something."

' "I'm sorry," Donnie frowned, "I was just playing."

"You play outside. In here, you stay in my office and color or play with your toys until it's time to go home."

"Okay. Are you mad at me?"

"Nah, little man. I can't be mad at you. Now please, apologize to the lady." Donnie hugged the manager's legs and softly apologized to Brenda.

"Don't worry about the mug," the manager told the cashier and Brenda as he walked away with Donnie in his arms. Brenda stood there shocked, still unable to utter a word. The cashier just gave her a strange look and continued to clean up the broken mug. "He didn't even seem fazed by my being here," Brenda thought. Her eyes welled up with tears when it dawned on her that Donnie could be his son. She slowly placed the shopping basket on the ground and quickly ran back to the cab, blinking back tears. When she returned to the cab, she told Tom that she couldn't find what she was looking for and that it was time for her to be home.

Brenda wondered if Tom knew who the manager was and about the history she had with him. She hoped he hadn't taken notice of her distress when she came running out of the store. On their way to her parent's house, Brenda remembered their last conversation—an unpleasant one. Although she had come back to Mayville to win his heart back, she was afraid that it was much too late already. After all, it had been almost 4 years since that last conversation. Unfortunately for Brenda, her life was not a walk in the park and through the years, came to regret many things. She'd always wondered if things had turned out the same for him.

Facing Andrew

The cab pulled up in front of the Jones' property. The large single-family home was located at the very end of a street lined with trees full of luscious leaves. The house was a light blue color with a large white porch. Brenda's parents did an exceptional job with the upkeep of their property. The porch was clean, the grass was green and their bushes were trimmed. She thanked Tom and sent her greetings to his parents as she stepped out of the cab. She looked up at their home and smiled. She closed her eyes and inhaled; she could already smell her mother's cooking. Brenda knocked on the door and her parents were the first to greet her. Her father; a bulky man with salt and pepper hair, a clean, shaven face was the first to hug her.

"There's my favorite girl! She's finally home," her father said happily. Then, her mother; a frail looking petite woman with blonde hair in a bun, embraced her and they remained like so for a few minutes. Eventually, their hug was interrupted by other family members who had joined them for Brenda's homecoming dinner. Brenda's aunts from her father's side were there and her cousins, Sara, Mary, Glenn and Duane, were there as well, they had come from another town almost an hour away from Mayville. Also in attendance, were a few family friends that had been around since before she was even born. Lastly, her sister, Elaine, came to greet her. She gave her a loose hug and kind of went on her way after that. It was no secret that Elaine resented Brenda for leaving the family to live in the city. The two sisters were close before Brenda's departure but things changed after she had left. Usually, Brenda would make a comment about Elaine's attempts to guilt-trip her but she was still overwhelmed from the incident at the store.

"Mama, I'm going to go upstairs to get cleaned up real quick before we start to eat, okay?" Brenda told her mother.

"Go ahead, hon. We know it's a long trip from the city," her mother replied and motioned her towards the stairs. Once upstairs, Brenda went into the bathroom and sat in the toilet. She quietly started to cry out the tears she had been holding back since she was at the store. Brenda regretted coming back to face her mistakes. She did not regret coming back; she wanted to. She regretted ever making the decision to move to the city and leave behind her friends and family, even though they were all against it. She had been in the bathroom for some time when a knock echoed through the bathroom.

"Who is it?" she called out.

"Brenda, it's mom. Is everything alright?" her mother asked concerned.

Brenda cracked the door open and said, "I saw Andrew."

"Andrew Mills?"

"Yes, mama. Andrew Mills." She opened the door to let her mother into the bathroom and shut the door behind her. "He didn't even care that he saw me."

"How do you know he didn't care? I'm sure he was just as shocked to see you as you were him. Where did you see him?" Then, Brenda recounted the events that took place at the store and her mother replied, "Brenda, it's been a long time. Maybe he was unable to process it at the moment."

"I guess," Brenda said, "what am I even doing? I messed everything up. It's too late for me to try to fix things."

"Don't say that, Brenda. It's never too late. And even if he doesn't want anything to do with you, at least you tried. At least you apologized. Before you were his girlfriend, you were really good friends. Surely, he remembers all those years of friendship," her mother said as she stroked Brenda's blonde bob.

"What should I do?"

"Do what you said you would do when you came back. Apologize to him for behaving the way you did back then." The thought of Andrew rejecting her apology made her unnerved. It almost made her not want to face him. However, she was determined to set the record straight with Andrew. Her mother told her that she should compose herself and join the family for dinner. She also suggested that Brenda not let any more time pass before she said something to Andrew. They agreed that Brenda would visit Andrew first thing in the morning and for the rest of the evening, Brenda and her family played poker, ate and danced. Brenda couldn't comprehend how her family could welcome her with such open arms after the way she left them. She left them and let herself believe that she deserved better than Mayville and the people there. As horrible as she had been, she prayed that Andrew also welcomed her with such warmth.

The next day, Brenda fixed herself up and got dressed and was well on her way before her parents and her sister woke up. She took the keys to her father's truck and drove the five miles to the store. Once she was there, she hesitated getting out of the car but she pushed herself to just get it over with. She walked inside and asked the first cashier in sight to speak to the manager. The cashier was a woman about the age of Brenda, she had light brown curly hair and eyes the color of honey. Brenda was taken aback by how stunning this woman was.

"Who is looking for him?" the cashier asked cheerily.

"Um, Brenda Jones." When Brenda said her name, the woman's expression changed dramatically. Her smile faded into a frown and she glared at Brenda, making her feel uneasy.

She turned and began to walk away and said, "Andrew isn't here and I really don't think he wants to see you."

"Oh, okay. Thank you," Brenda said meekly. The woman cashier had disappeared into one of the isles and Brenda was left standing there more stunned than angry at the woman's bluntness. She had a feeling that the cashier knew all about her but why did she seem so upset as if the matter was personal? Brenda wanted to waste no time in asking the strange woman so she started to make her way out of the store and towards Andrew's house. Andrew's house was only 3 blocks away from the store so she arrived at his small house in under 5 minutes. She parked across the street from his house; a small olive green single-family home with a wooden porch. Brenda sat in the truck unsure of what she was about to do. She thought about the little boy, Donnie, and was still curious about his relationship with Andrew. If that was his son, then maybe he had a wife at home as well. She didn't want to cause him any more problems but it's not like she's going to ask him to take her back, she tried to convince herself. All she wanted was to apologize and she knew there was no harm in that. However, the words the cashier told her back at the store kept repeating themselves in her mind. She was afraid that maybe he would be mean. "Why should he be nice to me?" Brenda asked.

A knock on her window startled her, causing her to jump. It was Andrew motioning her to roll down her window. When she rolled it down he asked, "Are you stalking me?"

"What? Stalking you? Oh no, I'm not, I was just—,"

"One of my employees just called to say that you were looking for me," Andrew cut her off.

"Yes, I went to look for you there first."

"So, are you just going to sit out here and watch my house?"

"No, I actually came to talk to you."

"Alright. Well, we can talk on my porch." And Brenda opened the truck door and followed Andrew by to a wooden swing on his porch. He sat down on the other end of the swing and looked ahead not saying a word. Before she thought of speaking, Brenda examined her former lover's face. Andrew didn't look like the seventeen year old boy she had left behind those 4 years ago. His face was still quite handsome but more mature. He sat up straight with his back against the back of the swing which allowed Brenda to see how much more broader his shoulders were.

"You came looking for me to talk, didn't you? Are you just going to sit there and stare?" Andrew asked her sharply. Brenda was caught off-guard by his question and blushed.

"I'm sorry," she replied softly as she brushed her hair away from her face, "it's been a really long time since I last saw you."

"Yeah, I guess it has," Andrew answered before going quiet again.

"I'm sorry about the whole thing with the little boy at the store. I didn't know he was yours."

"He's mine but he's not my son, if that's what you came here to ask. Donnie is Betty's son."

"Wait, Donnie is the baby Betty was expecting when I left?" Andrew nodded.

"Wow. How *is* Betty?" Andrew remained quiet for a moment before answering, "She's dead."

Betty was Andrew's older sister by 3 years. Betty was really good friends with Elaine and would come over their house every evening after school. Brenda loved Betty. Betty had introduced her to all the boy bands she grew to love. Brenda didn't expect that kind of response. Never in a million years would she have imagined that Betty would be dead. Her eyes welled up with tears at the thought of the pain her sister went through from losing her best friend. Brenda's heart sunk when she realized that Andrew lost his only sibling and she was not there for him.

"What happened?" She asked through tears. Thus, he began telling Brenda how she died right after childbirth and her deadbeat boyfriend disappeared from the hospital never to be heard from again leaving Donnie in the care of Andrew and his aunt. The aunt, however, was much too sickly to raise a child. Andrew became Donnie's guardian at the age of 18 and raised him all on his own. By the time Andrew finished telling Brenda everything she was weeping. Andrew was also teary-eyed and scooted to sit next to her. He put his arm around her shoulders and she leaned into his chest. Andrew wrapped his arms around her and allowed her to mourn her friend who had been deceased for over three years.

When Brenda was all out of tears, Andrew pulled away from her and said, "Everything's okay now, Brenda."

"Why didn't anybody tell me? Why didn't you call me?" Brenda cried.

"Honestly, Brenda. I didn't want to see you. You were the only person I wanted beside me but at the same time I was so mad at you. I didn't want to see your face. I asked your family to not say a word about Betty's death to you. I didn't want you to come back out of pity."

"How could you do that, Andrew? Are you really that prideful?" Brenda snapped at him.

"Hold up. Wait a minute, Brenda. You leave to the city and a few weeks later, you break up with me by phone and *you're* getting mad at *me*?" Andrew said standing up.

"Betty *died*. I should have been at her funeral. I should have been able to say goodbye."

"Well she was my sister. My sister had just passed. I thought, maybe you were just too busy with your new and improved life in the city. You left me even though I begged you not to leave. Maybe you shouldn't have left, Brenda. If you're here it's because life didn't go as you had planned. All those years; wasted."

"I'm just trying to make things right," Brenda whispered.

"I get that, I do. I just don't know if I can ever get over the way you behaved. If you'll excuse me, I have to get ready for work," Andrew said making his way towards the door. Brenda was left sitting on the porch alone. She calmly stood up and walked back to her truck and made her way back home. The regret she had come back home to was even greater now. She made sure she drove away from Andrew's house before bursting into more tears. Now more than ever, she lamented every leaving Mayville and the people who loved her behind.

Love & Basketball

After the talk Brenda had with Andrew, she was unwilling to try and talk to him again. She could not bare the thought of Andrew's ultimate rejection and banishing her from his life. She was at a loss about what to do because she loved Andrew but she didn't want him to think that she only came back to settle for less than what she truly wanted. Brenda decided to give him some space so she went about her days as she normally would in Mayville. There was not much to do in the small town, although, she was considering a job in the town's public middle school as a health teacher. She hadn't played much basketball since she graduated from college and suddenly got the urge to play.

Mayville had a park in the center near the schools. It was not by any means an elaborate park; it had a set of swings, a small jungle gym and a sandbox. There was also a basketball court and that was it for Mayville's park.

One evening, right before dinner, Brenda took her basketball and headed to the park. The sun was almost set and there was nobody at the park anymore so she had the court all to herself. She shot a couple of free throws and dribbled around the court. She stopped what she was doing when she heard voices coming towards her. Donnie ran up to her and said, "Can I play?"

"Sure you can, cutie," Brenda replied handing him the basketball. Andrew ran up behind him and waved at Brenda. She smiled at him. Donnie handed the ball to Andrew, signaling him to shoot it into the basket. Andrew threw it but missed.

"Haven't gotten any better, I see," Brenda laughed.

"Oh, be quiet," Andrew said laughing as well. Donnie picked up the ball and Andrew walked over to carry him and guide him to the basket. Once Donnie put it through the basket Andrew and Brenda celebrated while the toddler clapped for himself. They didn't talk much throughout their time at the park. Donnie was having a blast while Brenda attempted to teach him how to dribble. Andrew had never been that great at basketball and just stood to the side, watching everything that Brenda did. Donnie seemed to like her very much. They both ran around and laughed the entire time. Brenda found it hard to believe that Donnie was Betty's child. She wished she had been there when he had been born. Eventually, the child raised his arms for Andrew to pick him up and rubbed his sleepy eyes.

"It's close to little man's bedtime. I think we should go," Andrew said.

"Yeah, I agree. You don't want him to get overtired or something," Brenda replied.

"Thank you, Brenda. I'll see you around," Andrew said as they began to depart. At that moment, Brenda didn't want him to walk away. She wanted to tell him that she loved him and that she regretted the hurt she caused him but she couldn't say that. Instead she said,"Wait. That was fun. Let's do it again. Tomorrow, same time."

Andrew looked at Donnie and asked,"You want to do it again, buddy?"

Donnie clapped and giggled, "Again!" Andrew and Brenda laughed and agreed to meet at the basketball court the next day. Soon, Brenda was on her way home for dinner with a smile from ear to ear. Brenda, Andrew & Donnie met at the court every day to play basketball. Brenda and Andrew didn't speak much to each other during their play time. Brenda held off on speaking not because she didn't want to; she just didn't know what to say. It didn't matter that Andrew never said anything to her, though. She was just glad that he allowed her to spend time with him and his nephew. Regardless of the minimal exchange of words, all three always went home exhausted from all the fun they had.

On one particular night, Brenda arrived at the park to find that nobody was there. *Maybe they're running late.* After about fifteen minutes she was worried that nobody was going to show up. After all, Andrew's place was not that far from the park. She decided to wait a bit longer but with every passing minute her heart sank a little more. Just when she had decided to start heading home a pitter-patter of feet came up behind her. It was Donnie and he held up a red rose to her.

"For me?" Brenda asked relieved.

"Take it, Brenda," Donnie giggled.

"Thank you, little gentleman. How sweet of you," she gushed as she smoothed his hair with her hand. Andrew stood behind Donnie smiling at their interaction.

"Donnie, why don't you ask Miss Brenda what we talked about."

Donnie nodded and asked, "Miss Brenda, can you eat with us?"

"Right now?" she asked.

"Yes," Andrew replied, "we'd like for you to please join us for dinner. I mean, if you can and are willing to."

"Yeah, of course," Brenda quickly answered ,not caring about whether she sounded too eager. Truthfully, she was eager. She was eager to tell him what she had said long before. She was eager to demonstrate that she meant it, too.

She excused herself as she entered into their small home. It was just as she had always imagined Andrew would keep his place—organized and fresh-looking. Donnie grabbed her hand as she looked around and pulled her towards a toy chest in the living room. He started pulling out cars and lining them up in front of her. Brenda sat next to him.

"I'm going to finish up dinner, okay? Donnie, you be good. Don't forget to wash your hands, little man. And don't give Miss Brenda a hard time," Andrew instructed Donnie.

"Don't worry. We'll be good. You know I've never been much of a trouble maker," Brenda said through a smile. Andrew smiled back and excused himself into the kitchen.

"I'll be quick," he said as he disappeared past the doorway.

It was not long before Andrew called them both the dinner table. It was all set and ready for them to eat. Andrew had baked a hen with cranberry sauce and roasted carrots and Brussels sprouts. "Wow, it smells and looks delicious," Brenda complimented him. She had no idea that Andrew could even cook. That detail made him seem so much more attractive. She thought he was already attractive enough by his appearance and by the way he was obviously good with children. In her mind she asked herself how she even had the courage to leave behind such a dreamy guy.

As they dined at the dinner table, they mostly spoke about Donnie and his favorite things. Although he was only 3 years old, he was able to carry a conversation quite effortlessly. Brenda was impressed at how Andrew had raised him—gentle, intelligent, kind, curious. The thought of Andrew fathering her own children made her blush and it made her feel a little silly. *He'll probably never see me like that ever again.* They carried on with their conversation and talked through dessert as well which was a lemon meringue pie. By the time they were finished, it was time for Donnie's bath. Brenda agreed to wait in the living room while Andrew got Donnie ready for bed. Brenda sat on the couch next to an end table. There was a white wooden frame on the end table with Betty's picture in it. It was a picture of her on the porch swing smiling and holding up her hand in a peace sign. She looked radiant, just how Brenda remembered her. Wedged on the side of the frame was a baby picture, Brenda guessed it was Donnie from the button nose and wide eyes. Brenda held the frame in her hand and reminisced about all the things she did with Elaine and Betty. Life sure did change a lot in the time that she was gone. After all, 4 years was a very long time.

Rekindled

Brenda waited on the couch for maybe a half hour before Andrew came back out of Donnie's room.

"Hi," he said in a low-tone voice.

"Is Donnie asleep?"

"Yup. He is *out*," he laughed, "he has so much fun with you. And I guess I do, too."

"I have fun as well," Brenda blushed. Andrew sat next to her on the couch and grabbed her hand.

"Thank you. You're so nice to Donnie. I really appreciate that," he told her.

"No, *thank you* for allowing me to be a part of his life and yours even though I truly do not deserve it. I ruined everything when I left four years ago. You mourned your sister all alone and you had to raise her baby at the same time. I can't imagine the pain you went through. I should have been here to grieve alongside you."

"But you came back. Why?"

"Andrew, I've made so many mistakes in these past years. I shouldn't have left you behind. I could have asked you to come with me or at least made more of an effort to keep our relationship strong. Once school and basketball got busy, I let that take over my entire life because I wanted to be better than Mayville. But that was so dumb of me, because that was like saying that I wanted to be better than you, and my parents and Elaine and Betty."

"What happened in the city? Was it so bad? I mean, you got the chance to do what you love."

" I did make many accomplishments in the city, graduating and making it to women's basketball championships but I never felt like I truly belonged. I loved the experience but I just felt like maybe I soured my experience by pushing aside the things that truly mattered like you and my family."

"Do I still matter?" Andrew asked staring into her eyes so deeply that she almost forgot to respond.

"You've always mattered. What these 4 years have taught me is that you will always matter." She put her hand on his cheek and he placed his hand over hers.

"You have no idea how many times I had this dream where we are exactly how we are right at this very moment. I want to stay here frozen in this moment."

"We've already lost 4 years. I don't want frozen moments. I want to live them all with you," Brenda smiled, "Andrew, I'm sorry for hurting you. I'm sorry for leaving you alone at such a dark time in your life. I'm sorry for thinking that I was too good for our home here in Mayville." Andrew softly placed his hand on her neck and pulled her in for a kiss. Brenda melted right into him, just like in their younger days. She looked into his eyes and smiled.

"I love you, Andrew," she whispered.

"And I love you," Andrew replied, kissing her on the forehead. "We have so much time to make up. I was so tired of being mad. I wished every night that you would come back and we'd make up. I didn't want to believe that it was over."

Brenda kissed him again and told him, "Never. I'm here to stay. I want to be with you. I love Mayville, I love you, I love the people here. I love the simple life we live here. I want to live it here with you and with Donnie, if you want me to."

"There's nothing my heart desires more than that."

They laid on the couch and talked about their lives for hours. Brenda told him what it was like in the city and Andrew told her about all of the crazy things that had happened in Mayville since she had left. He told her about what it was like being Donnie's father figure and bragged about how smart and amazing he was. They did not even notice that they had begun to drift off to sleep—both laid out on the couch in an embrace. That was just one of the many nights that they shared with each other. Some nights Donnie was right there, cuddling with them. Brenda found a new kind of happiness from her hometown of Mayville. She had come to appreciate the simplicity of everyday life there. There was no traffic, no superficial and money-hungry people. She was surrounded by a tight-knit community who openly welcomed her back and not hordes of strangers just rushing to get to their jobs on time. In Mayville, time passed slowly. There was always time to bask in the moment and not have to worry about busy itineraries.

Brenda became a teacher at the public middle school where she made many friends amongst the rest of the faculty. Most of them were childhood friends of hers and some were even teachers she had when she herself was a student there. Brenda had also become close to her sister, Elaine, once again. Soon, Brenda had asked her to be her maid of honor at her wedding where they made a toast in honor of Betty for brightening up their lives with the most wonderful child who was loved by Andrew and Brenda like they eventually loved their very own children.

BETWEEN NOW AND HEAVEN

PHYLLIS ROGERS

Iris Quinn's body lay nearly comatose on the cold, sterile bed at Boston General Hospital. She had skipped her insulin doses in recent days, and her diabetes was out of control. She believed that medication was too expensive and a waste of money on someone of her advanced age. She didn't see the point. Except for a couple of acquaintances and the caretaker who went to her home a few times a week, she had no one left in the world. She was lonely and ready to move on from her earthly existence.

"We're losing her," Dr. Patel shouted in an exasperated tone. "I'm not getting a heartbeat on the monitor. Get the paddles," he ordered.

Iris saw her lifeless body below her as her essence seemed to drift up from her form. She felt no distress as she watched the medical personnel fight to save her life. She was caught between two worlds. She was filled with a sense of peace. All at once, Iris found herself back in time as memories of times past filled her vision.

The year was 1947, a couple of years after the war had ended. Nineteen year old Iris stole away for a moment from her duties at her family's Italian restaurant to read a few stanzas from a book of poetry she had been immersed in.

Working in the restaurant wasn't her favorite thing to do, but she knew she fared better than so many who had to work in factories during that time. The restaurant named for her grandmother yielded her family a comfortable lifestyle. It was one of the more popular eateries in the small suburb of Boston.

Iris's grandmother, who was known by everyone as Nonna, started the restaurant when her daughter, Sophia, was a teenager. The three women were on their own as both Nonna and Sophia lost their husbands in each world war. Iris never really knew her father.

"Iris! Table eight has been waiting for you to take their order."

Sophia was loving, yet firm with Iris. She knew Iris often had her head in the clouds. The past few years were difficult, and Sophia understood Iris's desire to escape into her make believe world. However, Iris needed a dose of reality from time to time.

"Yes, Madre," Iris complied.

Iris lay her book down and went to greet her patrons.

"It took you long enough. We haven't got all night," said the female diner, unleashing her fangs on Iris.

"Uh, it's quite ok, Miss," interjected the male companion.

Iris was instantly attracted to the gentle Irish brogue of the man at the table. She couldn't help but notice he was handsome as well. He was a good ten years or more Iris's senior, but had a boyish charm about him. His dark brown hair was longer at the front and top; it was slicked to one side and held it in place with pomade. His light blue eyes seemed to smile along with his thin lips, which formed a slightly crooked grin.

"The special this evening is Veal Marsala," Iris informed them. "Of course, we have our regular menu items as well."

"I think the Veal Marsala sounds quite scrumptious," the Irishman told Iris as he nodded to his lady friend.

"Actually, I would prefer something more agreeable," the female companion replied testily. "I'd like something besides veal." She spoke in a vain and haughty manner, and seemed contrary to Iris. It was clear the woman would find fault with most anything.

"I'll have the Chicken Parmigiana," the lady said, almost barking her order to Iris.

Iris noticed throughout the evening that the gentleman seemed bored, and at times embarrassed by his female companion. She felt sorry for the Irish gent. She also felt relieved when they departed the restaurant so that she wouldn't have to put up with the woman any longer. She wouldn't have minded, though, listening to the male diner speak a little more. She fancied his accent. She imagined how wonderful it would sound to hear him recite some of the poetry in her book.

The next morning, Iris went out to the courtyard that was set to the side of the restaurant. They grew herbs in the courtyard for many of the dishes served in the restaurant. Flowers lined the paths as well and provided fresh blossoms for the tables of the restaurant. An old cast iron bench rested alongside the Marian statue that Nonna had brought with her from Italy. Iris took breaks as she cut herbs and flowers and laid the fresh bunches in the basket at her feet. The breaks afforded her opportunities to catch up on reading.

She opened her book of T.S. Elliot poems and continued to read where she had left off from the evening before, on Elliot's work, *The Wastelands*. She transcribed the German words from part one of the poem:

> "Fresh the wind blows
> Towards home
> My Irish child
> Where are you now?"

Her reading was interrupted by a familiar voice. The Irish gentleman from the evening before approached her from the street.

"Good day, Miss," he said to Iris as he tipped his hat. "I wanted to apologize for the rudeness of my companion last evening."

"Oh, really, it's quite ok. I'm sure your wife just had a bad day or something," Iris replied. She was surprised to see him again.

"Oh no, Miss. She wasn't my wife. My pal set us up for a date. I guess you can say it didn't go over very well."

Iris noticed it again. His slightly crooked smile was adorable and as charming as his accent.

"I'm Alister Quinn. I've just come from Ireland a few months ago. I'm the new editor at the Boston Herald, and I live in the flat just across the way there," he informed Iris as he pointed to the apartments not too far down the road.

"My mother and Nonna, my grandmother, own this restaurant. We live above it so I suppose we're neighbors," Iris said. "My name is Iris."

Alister noticed the book Iris was holding in her hands. "Perhaps you would like to accompany me to dinner near the harbor one day, and we can discuss his poetry," Alister said.

"I would like that very much," Iris agreed. She was intrigued that a man would consider her insight. "Sunday evening would be best," she suggested as the restaurant kept her busy most days.

It would become a ritual that the two of them would meet on Sunday evenings. They quickly became inseparable. They would steal moments during the week, usually with Alister sitting with her for a few minutes before work, on the garden bench. Their courtship lasted nine months. At last, Alister asked for her hand in marriage.

"*Mo Ghrá Eternal*?" It had become a term of endearment from Alister to Iris meaning *My Eternal Love*. They had just finished reading sonnets from Shakespeare. "Would you do me the honor of becoming Mrs. Alister Quinn?"

He had knelt down in front of the bench, and his fingers clutched a ring which had been his grandmother's. The ring was like none Iris had ever seen, fashioned in antique silver. Two hands held a heart with a crown on top, and there was an emerald stone inside the heart. *Mo Ghrá Eternal* was etched on the inside of the band.

Alister had already received a blessing from Iris's mother for Iris's hand in marriage. He was a proper gentleman and would have asked her father, had he still been alive.

"Yes," she shouted. She wanted nothing more at that moment. Iris couldn't be happier ...

"We have a heartbeat," Dr. Patel emphasized as he instructed the nurses to pause their efforts. Their mission was accomplished. Iris drew back from the brink of death.

She again found herself supine on the table at Boston General. Her body, her consciousness, whatever - she didn't know what had happened. She had relived one of the happiest moments of her life, but here she was, thrust back into the present.

She couldn't open her eyes, but she could hear everything around her. She was disappointed to have left her other state, whatever it was. She felt the weight of her body and the sorrows of her heart settle upon her once again. Unable to speak or move, she was not really troubled by it, and time passed without her notice.

***

With time, Iris came out of the diabetic-induced coma and was transferred out of ICU into a step-down room at the hospital. Dr. Patel had assessed her. He determined that the only lasting damage from her diabetic episode was to her eyes. Iris could no longer see very well. Everything was a blurry mess, and she couldn't focus on anything.

"Alright now, Mrs. Quinn. We have you all settled in your new room. My name is Nurse Douglass. If you need anything, here is the call button." She took Iris's hand and placed it over the device.

It was a scary and frustrating experience for Iris. Not only was she ill and alone, but having her vision so impaired just made matters worse. Now more conscious and aware, she felt her mood darken.

Iris guessed that Nurse Douglass was an African American woman, based on her warm voice tone and the texture of her skin when the nurse had grabbed her hand. During their initial, brief encounter, Nurse Douglass reminded Iris of her caretaker, Janice, whom Iris was quite fond of. Iris wondered if Janice or anyone had checked on her during her days in ICU?

"Code Blue to Room 214. Code Blue to Room 214." The loud call for help from the intercom jolted Iris, and she felt more frightened. She heard the frantic pacing of doctors and nurses rush past her door into a nearby room. She could see only shadows of the figures hurrying to answer the code.

The voices of the medical personnel faded into the background as Iris felt panicked.

"You'll get used to it after a while," a male voice promised.

Iris had not noticed anyone else in the room before.

I must be in a semi-private room, she thought to herself. She found it strange that they would place her in a room with a man rather than a woman. She noticed a shadow to her left which she suspected was a curtain used to provide more privacy.

The voice reminded her of her beloved, Alister. She detected a faint accent which sounded Irish, but the gentleman's voice was softer and older than Alister's.

"Are you well enough to read?" the gent inquired. "It could help take your mind off of things while you are here."

"I'm...I can't see very well anymore," Iris informed him. "I'm losing my vision." Iris's voice sounded weak and frail.

"I can read to you, if you'd like," the man offered. Iris nodded in appreciation.

The gentleman read from a book of poetry which included many of the famous poets of the nineteenth and early twentieth centuries. He read her some of Keats' work, as Alister had so many years ago.

> *"Bright star, would I were stedfast as thou art—*
> *Not in lone splendour hung aloft the night*
> *And watching, with eternal lids apart,*
> *Like nature's patient, sleepless Eremite,*
> *The moving waters at their priestlike task*
> *Of pure ablution round earth's human shores,*
> *Or gazing on the new soft-fallen mask*
> *Of snow upon the mountains and the moors..."*

Iris relaxed, the gentle readings calming her troubled spirit. The voice of the gentleman remained eerily familiar. Though she was entranced by the words he spoke, the medications took over her tired body, and she fell asleep as his voice faded into the night.

***

The next morning, Iris awoke to the sounds of the morning medical staff making their rounds. Nurse Douglass arrived into Iris's room to tend to her needs.

"How are we feeling this morning, Mrs. Quinn?"

Iris shrugged one shoulder and reluctantly nodded. She wasn't sure how to answer.

"Well, I suppose I've been better, dear," Iris responded.

Nurse Douglass checked Iris's blood sugar.

"Hmmm... Still elevated a bit," she said with disappointment. "We're going to have figure out what to do with you," the nurse said as she exited the room.

The day seemed so long to Iris. She wondered what would become of her life. How would she manage when she left the hospital? Would she even leave the hospital? There were so many questions and so few answers.

She tried to pray away her fears, but felt so weak and afraid. The gentleman in her room sensed her distress and offered to read to her again.

"Psalms always helped to calm my beloved wife's fears. Would it be okay if I read them to you?"

"Please." Iris was thankful to hear the elder man's voice again.

"Even when I walk
through the darkest valley,
I will not be afraid,
for you are close beside me.
Your rod and your staff
protect and comfort me."

The words comforted and soothed Iris's weary soul. She remembered how she and Alister read verses from Song of Solomon on their wedding day. She told the story of her love for Alister to the stranger on the other side of the curtain.

"We were married on St. Patty's Day. Alister and I had both been raised Catholic and attended the same cathedral down the road from us, but somehow had never seen each other until the day when he came to our restaurant. Perhaps it was because my Nonna always insisted we arrive a half hour early prior to each service. She ushered us to the very front pew as though the spot was reserved for us. She would say that to be at the very front was like being at the feet of God."

"I wore the same wedding dress that my Madre had worn to her wedding. Nonna styled my black hair and clipped a large hair comb to the front side of my head. The comb was very beautiful and very old. It had three large sapphire stones, and Nonna said it was a perfect match for my blue eyes. She said the two together looked like the waters of the deepest ocean."

"My Alister was dashing as ever. I couldn't take my eyes off of him as I walked down the aisle. I wish I could say that I remembered what he wore, but I just remember his tilted smile and his eyes. We did not glance away from each other. Our eyes were fixed in anticipation that I would soon be Mrs. Alister Quinn."

"We read verses from Song of Solomon in our vows to each other. It had become an almost nightly ritual that we would recite excerpts from the book, so it seemed only natural to include them in our promise to each other."

"My beloved has gone down to his garden,
To the beds of balsam,
To pasture his flock in the gardens
And gather lilies.
I am my beloved's and my beloved is mine,
He who pastures his flock among the lilies."

"The church spilled over with people. We were popular in our district of Boston. Everyone knew our restaurant and had dined there, so there were many guests there to wish me well. I always felt sad for my Alister because he had a few of his friends and mostly people from the newspaper, but he had no family to speak of there to bless him in his new life. He never really shared with me why. I suppose I should have asked. I always figured, perhaps, that it was too expensive for his family to come to America."

"Perhaps it was enough for him to be where he was with you and your family became his family?" The gentleman had interrupted Iris's narrative of her life with Alister.

"Maybe," Iris conceded. "I hope we helped to fulfill his life. I know he did mine."

The gentleman smiled and nodded at Iris, and though she could not see it, she sensed it.

Iris continued with her story of her new life with Alister.

"Madre and Nonna prepared all of the food for our reception. It seemed only fitting to receive the wedding guests at our family restaurant. We had plenty of room to accommodate everyone, and extra tables were set outside in the garden terrace. Oh, it was so lovely. The wedding was in late May and all of the spring flowers were bursting at the seams."

"Our reception was lively and entertaining. Alister had sung with a couple of other Irish lads in the pubs they ventured to before our courtship. He'd often serenade me with songs from his homeland."

"When I told him his eyes smiled at me just the same as his crooked grin, he introduced me to the song he would eventually sing at our wedding reception. It quickly became of favorite of mine and it was *our song*. He managed to work up the courage to sing it to me in front of all our guests, and as he did, he twirled me around the dance floor."

Iris began to faintly sing the chorus to the song she had heard Alister sing to her often. With her weakened voice, it was more of a whisper that filled her hospital room.

"When Irish eyes are smiling,
sure 'tis like a morn in spring.
In the lilt of Irish laughter,

you can hear the angels sing.
When Irish hearts are happy,
all the world seems bright and gay,
And when Irish eyes are smiling,
sure, they steal your heart aw..."

Iris's voice faded. She had used all of her strength during the emotional recounting of her life. She felt somewhat breathless and tired, and panted a little. Nurse Douglass walked into her room just in a time to catch a glimpse of Iris's struggle to take a deep breath.

"Mrs. Quinn! How long have you been this way?"

"Not very long dear. I think I just excited myself."

Nurse Douglass checked Iris's oxygen levels. Her frown deepened as she fit the oxygen mask over Iris's face.

"Try to take a few deep breaths."

The nurse felt Iris's wrist and took her pulse and blood pressure. She felt satisfied that Iris was stabilizing after a few minutes of oxygen.

"I'll be in to check on you more often this evening. In the meantime, remember the call button is there for a reason," she reminded Iris as she wrapped Iris's hand around the cylindrical apparatus.

The nurse gave Iris more of the medication that made her sleepy. She drifted off once again.

***

Iris grew more tired in the coming days. She wondered if the man who had kept her company all those days in the hospital was still with her in the room.

"Hello," Iris called out. "Are you still there?"

"I'm here," the elderly chap acknowledged. "I think they want you to remain calm, so I didn't want to disturb you."

"Rubbish," Iris said. "Maybe I'm too weak to talk much, but you can talk to me. I want to know more about you."

"I'm not sure where to start," the old guy told Iris.

"Why don't you start from the beginning?"

"Well, I was a wee boy in Dublin."

Iris knew it. His accent wasn't as robust as Alister's, but it resembled it still the same.

"I lived with my Nanna, who was my Mum's Mum. My Mum and Pops struggled to make ends meet while my Nanna watched over me. God rest her soul. She was a good part of my life when I was younger, she and my Mum. But Mum's life was hard."

"Pops worked hard, but we couldn't seem to get anywhere. He was upset all the time and drank a lot. The more he drank, the meaner he got."

Iris's new friend paused.

"I don't think I should be telling you this. I don't want to upset you."

"No, please. I want to hear about it," Iris said. "Go on."

"When my Pops wasn't drinking, he could be the kindest man. But when he was drunk, things could get out of hand. He'd hit my Mum, sometimes he'd hit me. My Mum or my Nanna often got between Pops and me to protect me."

"One night, he was smoking in the chair and fell asleep. The chair caught fire and burned the house down with it. My Mum and I made it out, but Nanna and Pops died in the fire. I had a small cloth sack with a couple of treasures in it that my Nanna had given me that I always wore around my neck. I always had that to remind me of her. Everything else was destroyed in the fire."

"We stayed with relatives until my Mum found a way for us to be on our own. It took a while, but she did. Mum always found a way. I never knew what she did then, but I have my suspicions now."

"It was pretty rough, growing up in Ireland. It was a beautiful place, but it was filled with so much turmoil. I was good in my studies and worked to better myself. I always said I would be a better man than my

Pops, and if I ever was blessed with children, I would never treat them in a bad way. And if I were ever fortunate enough to find the love of good woman, she would save me from the wretched life I came from."

"Somehow, I made it to America and was determined to start a new life. After school, I worked my way up at my job, and became successful. But I still had a hole in my heart. I wanted someone to love and to love me."

"One day, I found her. I found my angel, and we got married. And.."

Iris had fallen asleep again. They had her on stronger medications, and she didn't have the strength to fight their effects.

Nurse Douglass had come in to check on Iris regularly. She was growing fond of her. She noticed Iris had relaxed her grip on the call button and went to move her hand near it again. She noticed the beautiful Claddagh ring around Iris's finger.

"Something tells me that your life has a story, Mrs. Quinn," she whispered as she pulled the covers higher over Iris's tiny and shrunken body.

***

Despite their best efforts, the doctor still struggled to gain control of Iris's diabetes. One problem would be solved, but the medications often complicated another. It was an exhausting process for both the doctor and Iris.

A few days turned into weeks at the large hospital. Iris continued to sleep a lot. Each time she awakened, she wondered if her roommate was still there. And each time, he was.

"Last thing I remember was you telling me about your hardships in Ireland," Iris told her friend. "I know much of what I've told you of my life has seemed idyllic compared to yours. But I want you to know, you weren't alone in the tragedies of life. Alister and I experienced our heartbreaks as well."

She could see the shadow of the man move closer to her. She couldn't make out any distinguishing features. Her eyesight had grown worse in recent days, and she had very little vision left.

"Let's see. Where did I stop last time?" she asked.

"You had just gotten married," her friend reminded her.

"Oh yes," Iris acknowledged.

"Alister and I moved in a place just across the way from the restaurant, but I still helped my Madre and Nonna. That is until..."

"Until?" The man echoed after Iris paused.

"Until our son, Danny, was born." Iris had a strange look on her face. It was one of many emotions, as if she wasn't sure which she should feel.

"When Danny was born, our lives changed. I had not known how complete a child could make our lives. We had already felt complete when we found each other, Alister and I. But a child brought something to our hearts that we didn't know was possible. We loved someone much more than ourselves. At last, I understood my Madre and Nonna."

"Alister doted on our little Danny. Alister wanted to name him 'Danny' in honor of his grandmother. He said she'd sing the song, *Danny Boy*, when Alister was sad or afraid."

"Alister was a lot more hands-on than most fathers of his time. He'd steal away moments from work early in the afternoons to get home and spend more time with our little Danny. He'd read to him, fly paper planes he had made for him, and he'd tell him that one day, they would fly across the world together. He did all sorts of things. Of course, he sang to him too. I guess you know which song he sang," Iris said as she chuckled and felt alive for a moment.

"One day, our lives were turned upside down. America was in the midst of the polio epidemic, and despite our best efforts to keep him safe, our Danny got it."

"He was seven years old, and one day couldn't get out of bed. Alister had taken Danny to fly a kite just the day before. He was so excited when had come home from their day in the wide open field. I remember him running through the garden gate and yelling 'Madre, Madre! Papi and I flew the kite into the air. It went so high! Almost as high as the clouds. You should have seen it!'"

"I remembered thinking I would go with them next time. There would always be other times, so I'd thought. The next morning, our little Danny was paralyzed down one side."

Iris began to weep with what little strength she had. Her roommate made tiny whimpering sounds as well.

"Save your strength," he cautioned her, his voice breaking slightly. "I think we need to let this rest for now."

Iris had no choice. Remembering the devastating moment in her family's life had taken all of her strength.

Nurse Douglass came into her room and saw that Iris had been crying.

"Oh my word! What's got you all upset, dear lady?"

She dabbed Iris's cheeks with tissue and brushed her thinning gray hair back away from her worn and wrinkled face. The compassionate nurse put her hand on top of Iris's hand and told her "Iris. I have you on my heart each day when I come in here and each day when I leave. I don't know what God's plan for you is, but I know this."

Nurse Douglass put one hand under Iris's and clasped the top of her hand.

"He's got you in the palm of His hand. It will all be okay."

Iris once again was quick to fall asleep after getting her medication.

Nurse Douglass felt bad for her. During Iris's stay, she had only noticed one visitor and that was early in Iris's treatment. She was too sick then to notice or remember. Nurse Douglass was told it was Iris's caretaker, but the visitor had not returned.

How sad, Nurse Douglass thought, *that anyone should be that alone.*

***

During her next moments of lucidness, Iris continued to tell her story to the man she could sense was only a few feet from her.

"At first, the polio didn't affect Danny's breathing much. He had spent a good bit of time at the hospital learning how to walk again. He could walk some, but it was easier for him to just be in a wheelchair. So when he came home, he was more confined than he had been before polio took over his body."

"Alister had built ramps that helped Danny get around better. Otherwise, he tried to treat Danny much like he had before he was sick, although perhaps was a little more overprotective. Alister would carry Danny out to the field so that they could fly kites. During days when the winds were kinder, he'd hand Danny a reel and help him hold it in his hands as they flew the kite. I went with them on those days. I had learned every moment was precious, and nothing could be taken for granted."

"Winter had come, and the doctors somehow felt the cool air would help Danny feel stronger and aid in his recovery. So, they would have us sit him out in the cold air a few minutes on days that we were able."

"We were always cautioned that Danny had lungs that were weaker than they should be because of the polio and that a small cold could set him back and even force him to spend time on an iron lung to be able to breathe."

Iris took a deep breath, exhausted in her tale of her son's health crisis.

"Influenza was spreading through Boston as was a massive snow storm. Everything was shut down. It was hard to get from one place to another. The flu was hitting whole families at a time, and it made its arrival to our house. It knocked us all down, but no one was harder hit than our Danny. We wanted to get him to the hospital, but it proved to be nearly impossible. Transportation was down. Communication lines were down. And we barely had the strength to walk from one room to another. Still, Alister and I took shifts at Danny's side, while we waited for conditions to improve. We had planned to get Danny to the hospital as soon as we could."

Tears fell from Iris's small, bloodshot eyes. She thought she heard the sound of a whimper come from her friend. They had grown very close and seemed to feel each other's pain. There was an unspoken bond which developed between them. There was even a love they felt for each other as they spent many hours in the dark hospital room.

"I walked into Danny's room, and Alister was sobbing. He was cradling our Danny's lifeless body and rocking back and forth. He wept until he could no more and then just stopped rocking, almost as if he was frozen in time."

"I had nearly collapsed on the chair on the far side of the room, unbeknownst to Alister, who was deep in his grief. Somehow, I managed to get myself up. I walked over to the two people I loved most in the world and wrapped my arms around both. It was my time to sob as I lost control of my emotions. And as I did so, Alister started singing the song he had sung to our son from the day he was born:

'Oh, Danny boy, the pipes, the pipes are calling
From glen to glen and down the mountain side
The summer's gone and all the roses falling
It's you, it's you, must go and I must bide
But come ye back when summer's in the meadow
Or when the valley's hushed and white with snow
It's I'll be here in sunshine or in shadow
Oh, Danny boy, oh, Danny boy, I love you so
But when ye come and all the flowers are dying
If I am dead and dead I well may be
You'll come and find the place where I am lying
And kneel and say an 'Ave' there for me...'"

Iris's friend had joined her in recanting the song by now, both gently singing barely above a whisper.

"And I shall hear tho' soft you tread above me
And all my grave will warmer, sweeter be
For you will bend and tell me that you love me
And I shall sleep in peace until you come to me."

"We cradled our son amidst the deafening silence that followed. We couldn't seem to will our bodies to move for what seemed like hours. Eventually, we did. I couldn't tell you when or how long we lay there on the bed with our son."

Iris grew silent. Her companion was silent also. No more words were spoken that evening in the hospital room, until at last, Iris drifted off to sleep.

***

The doctors were running out of options for Iris. They couldn't seem to get her diabetes under control, and there were signs that she was losing kidney function and declining rapidly.

In spite of it all, Iris felt no worse than she had been feeling. She was anxious for the conversations she had with her friend. Somehow, she felt he knew her heart and was able to glimpse at her soul.

"Eventually, it was time to move on without our Danny," Iris continued the story.

"You couldn't tell me that at the time. The loss of our little Danny nearly ended me. I locked myself away in my room, and stared out of the window into the distance."

"Alister tried to reach me in all sorts of ways. He would read sonnets of our favorite poetry. He would sing hymns or read verses from the Bible, particularly Psalms or Song of Solomon as he had always done."

"It fed my soul and somewhere within the depths of my being, it made me feel alive. But I didn't have the strength to pull out of my grief just yet."

"Alister never gave up on me and eventually, I came around and started living life again. It was a life without Danny. One day I realized poor Alister had to live it too. I had been selfish in my grief and had shut him out. It was time to try and move on. Alister saved me from myself. He saved me from the depths of despair. I don't know if he ever knew it, but he did."

"I have a feeling you saved him as well," her faithful companion told her.

"I don't know," Iris questioned. "When I think about it, there was so much I didn't know about his life before me and I should have asked. I was an open book."

"Maybe his life started when he met you," the old man reasoned. "Perhaps that is so?"

No one had been so encouraging to Iris since her Alister. She found herself once again comparing the similarities between her new friend and the love of her life.

If only for a brief moment, she felt young again and wondered if it was too late for love once more. She quickly put the thought out of her head. She was nearing eighty, and she would never allow herself to love another besides her beloved, Alister. She had a number of chances after his death, but always remained faithful to their love.

"Mo Ghrá Eternal - M'aingeal.."

Iris couldn't have heard what she just thought she did. *Maybe I'm hallucinating*, she thought. It was the voice of her friend using the terms of endearment that Alister had spoken to her on an almost daily basis. *Mo ghra eternal, M'aingeal* which translated meant *My Eternal Love, My Angel*. No one had ever spoken those words to her except for Alister. Iris couldn't recall telling the gentleman in her room about that. She questioned herself over and over again. She was on a lot of medications. Maybe she didn't remember telling him? Still, it was a bit unsettling.

"Did you just say something," she asked him.

Nurse Douglass walked in as Iris was speaking.

"Who are you talking to dear?"

"I was just asking my friend over there a question," Iris responded, still feeling a bit shaken.

Nurse Douglass's eyes widened, and she looked perplexed.

"Hmmm... There is no one here my dear but you and I," Nurse Douglass told Iris.

Iris gasped. "No! It can't be true. Why are you saying that?"

"It's ok Mrs. Quinn. Just calm down. We'll..."

Nurse Douglass noticed Iris's body grow limp. She checked her breathing and heartbeat and both were absent from Iris's body. She hit a button and called the code.

"Code Blue, Room 210, Code Blue, Room 210!" shouted Nurse Douglass as she started CPR on Iris.

Iris discovered herself again looking at her body from above. This time, there was a light and on each side were two figures. She moved closer to the light. She recognized the figures. There to take her home were Alister and Danny. There were no words spoken, but a language between them that transcended beyond the human comprehension. Iris's spirit knew then that the stranger in her room was her Alister, comforting her and preparing to take her home.

THE END

FOREVER

UNEXPECTED

58

MONICA MARKS

Bethany felt a sharp nudge at her ribs and she quickly blinked the sleep from her eyes, startled.

"Beth, look at that!" Andrea whispered, leaning across her half-awake frame to point out the tiny window. Bethany turned her head to look out the pane and her breath caught in her throat. The plane was descending over the most breathtaking landscape which she had ever seen.

That isn't saying much, Bethany thought with dry amusement. *This is the first time I have ever been out of Indiana in my life. Still, I can't imagine that it gets much more lovely than this.*

She watched as steaming mountaintops passed beneath them and they flew above lush, green jungles as far as the eye could see.

"Attention ladies and gentlemen," a flight attendant said over the intercom. "We will be landing in Managua in fifteen minutes. Please ensure that your trays are in the upright position and your seatbelts are fastened."

Bethany checked her waist quickly for the strap and sat back against the seat. The flight had been less scary than she had anticipated. She had rather enjoyed the journey through the clouds.

It's a little bit like being next to God, Bethany thought. She cast a sidelong look at Andrea who was still straining over her lap to take in the scenery.

She is so excited about this trip. I wonder why she does these missions so often. You would think she would be discouraged by the futility behind them. No matter how many supplies we send or hours we volunteer, the locals continued to be sick but the thousands. It's like ramming your head against a wall.

For Bethany's part, she had been basically blackmailed into joining the church group on that excursion. Pastor Frank had pulled her aside one afternoon after choir practice.

"Your voice has become more lovely with each passing year, Bethany," he told her appreciatively. "We are so blessed to have you in our choir."

"Thank you, Pastor," she replied, smiling demurely. She was pleased by the young Reverend's compliment. Like the other young ladies in the parish, she had somewhat of a school girl's crush on James Frank. He was still unmarried and there was a playful competition among the women to see who might be able to win his affections. Yet as the years melted by, it became apparent that Pastor Frank had no mind for marriage, at least not to any of the single women in his midst. Still, Bethany could not help but feel flattered by his kind words.

"Bethany, I wanted to ask you about something," Pastor Frank continued and Bethany turned her green eyes to stare up at him.

"Sure," she replied. "Ask away."

Pastor Frank cleared his throat and looked uncomfortably at his shoes. Bethany was immediately filled with a sense of caution.

Uh oh...is he speaking on behalf of my parents?

"We have a mission upcoming to Nicaragua," he said slowly, maintaining his gaze on the floor. Bethany was already shaking her dark hair. Every time a trip was planned to some God forsaken third world environment, he tried to recruit her. Bethany could think of nothing less appealing than spending two weeks in a suffocating country, encased in flies. It was not that Bethany was heartless. She volunteered at the church's soup kitchen every second weekend and worked as a camp counsellor with the developmentally challenged in the summer. Bethany was thrilled to help in any way she could; at home.

"Before you refuse, Bethany, I should tell you that we will be forced to cancel the trip if we don't find one more body. You have never gone on a mission, have you?"

"No, I haven't," Bethany agreed. "And I have no interest in going now."

Pastor Frank shook his head sadly.

"I know how you feel about these excursions, Bethany but I wouldn't be asking if you weren't my only hope."

Bethany gritted her teeth and stared at her hands. She knew that Jeanie Williams would typically be the sixth person to go but she had just had a baby. She wracked her brain for anyone else to replace Jeanie but she was coming up blank. She imagined that Pastor Frank had already done the same.

"I wouldn't be asking you if we had another option, Beth," Pastor Frank assured her. "I promise you, this will be a life changing experience for you. When you see the children's faces light up, it will all be worth it."

If I say no, they will cancel the trip and everyone will be angry at me, Bethany thought miserably. *There really isn't much of a choice, is there?*

Bethany sighed heavily.

"When do we leave?"

As the aircraft descended into the surreal beauty of Managua, Bethany could not help but feel a spark of excitement.

"I hope Dr. Martinez is still here," Andrea breathed as the landing gear touched the runway. "In all the missions I have ever done, he is the best doctor I have ever seen. The children love him and he is so caring."

Bethany rolled her eyes.

"He's a doctor, Andy. That's basically in his job description," she replied.

Andrea's eyes clouded over as she shook her head.

"You would think so," Andrea answered sadly. "But the stress of the job gets to most of them. The death and sickness turns what were probably great doctors into robots. I have been to countries where they treat their patients like an assembly line. One physician in Liberia actually would scream, 'next!' and shove the patient off the bed to make room for another. It was horrifying." Bethany was shocked but she was certain Andrea was exaggerating. Doctors were well paid for their roles. Why else would someone become a doctor?

"Ladies and gentleman, we have arrived in Managua, Nicaragua. The temperature here is a balmy 101 degrees and the sun is shining. We hope you had a pleasant flight aboard American Airlines flight 867 and we thank you for flying with us. Have a lovely stay in Nicaragua."

One hundred and one degrees? What kind of hell on earth have we flown into? Bethany thought woefully. Her mood was already souring at the thought of the heat.

Slowly, seatbelts came off and Andrea rose into the aisle to allow for Bethany to follow her onto the runway tarmac. The women blinked at the intense rays of sun as they descended the stairs. Bethany's legs were cramped from the four-hour flight and she realized she was thirsty.

"Do you have any water," she asked Andrea as they walked into the Augusto C. Sandino International Airport. Andrea nodded and dug a bottle from inside her carryon bag. Bethany took a swig and wiped her brow. She was already sweating.

They walked toward the luggage carousel to wait for their bags. The rest of their group had arrived the previous day with the supplies. Andrea and Bethany had been unable to get on that flight which was fine with Bethany. It just meant one less day that she would be stuck in Central America.

"Oh, there's one of yours, Beth," Andrea told her, gesturing at the bags. Instantly, a young boy appeared at her side. Bethany guessed him to be no older than eight. He was filthy and wore a flimsy, holey t-shirt. His knees were scarred and thin in a pair of shorts that were swimming trunks and much too large for his small form. His flip flops were as good as bare feet, they had eroded so badly. He offered Bethany and Andrea a bright smile.

"I help!" he declared, rushing to grab the bag.

"No, wait!" Bethany yelled but Andrea put her hand on her companion's arm and shook her head.

"Just let him get it," she whispered. "He's only looking to make a dollar."

Bethany was alarmed as she watched the frail boy struggle with the luggage. She rushed over to assist him with wrestling the bag over the belt. Panting, the child waved her away.

"I have," he told her. "More?"

Swallowing, Bethany nodded and pointed out their other belongings. The child refused any more help, almost knocking himself over with the heavy items.

He is too small to be doing this, she thought, but she did not interfere. She glanced at Andrea and she could see the compassion in the older woman's face.

When they had claimed their belongings, the boy piled up the mound and rolled behind them, still beaming happily. Bethany desperately wanted to sent the boy on his way but Andrea seemed content having him assist.

They cleared customs and exited the gate, the boy faithfully at their side.

"How long is he going to carry our bags?" Bethany finally whispered to Andrea, her heart breaking.

"Until they are loaded into a car safely," she replied calmly but Bethany could see she was as affected by the child's struggling as she.

Bethany clamped her mouth closed.

She has more experience in these things than I do but still...

"Andrea!" A tall, intelligent looking man was hurrying toward them, the beam on his tired face lighting the dusty airport. Andrea squealed in a childlike fashion, causing Bethany to give her a strange look. She had never seen her friend look so excited. The man approached and embraced Andrea warmly. He stepped back and Bethany examined him furtively.

Ah, this is probably the doctor she was talking about on the plane, Bethany thought, eyeing the handsome man. He wore thin green scrubs which were worn with age but it brought out the warm glow of his bronze skin and wavy black hair. His eyes were wide and cat-shaped with extremely long lashes, framing a set of intense, brown eyes. He was taller than Bethany expected, towering over both the women but at least six inches.

"Dr. Martinez, this is Bethany Grieger. This is her first mission anywhere so you will have to show her some extra attention," Andrea joked. The doctor rested his eyes on Bethany, his eyes lighting up as he stared at her expressive jade eyes.

"Welcome to Managua, Betany," he said cordially, offering her a long hand. "I hope this will not be your last trip with us."

Bethany accepted it, relishing his lilting accent and his inability to pronounce the "h" in her name.

"Nice to meet you, Dr. Martinez," she told him. Their gazes locked for a moment and time seemed to slow momentarily. He broke the spell, turning his attention the boy with the luggage.

"I see you have met Dario," he said, ruffling the child's hair. Dario smiled up at the doctor.

"Hola, doctor," Dario smiled. The two exchanged a few words in Spanish before Dr. Martinez gestured for the women to follow them

"Excuse me for speaking in our native tongue," he told them apologetically. "Dario's sister has been very sick and I wanted to know how she was doing. Unfortunately, his English is not fluent."

"What is wrong with his sister?" Bethany asked as they made their way back into the sunshine.

"She is suffering from cholera," Dr. Martinez answered sadly and Bethany gasped.

"Oh, how awful! How old is she?"

Dario began to load the bags into a beat-up VW bus, his smile never wavering.

"She is five but luckily she is on the upswing," Dr. Martinez replied. Dario finished heaving the luggage into the back of the van and turned to the group. Andrea already had a bill in her hand which she deposited into Dario's small palm. The boy looked at the crumpled paper in his hand, his mouth dropping open.

"Oh, gracias, senora! Muchas gracias!" he almost sobbed, clutching the money. His dark eyes were filled with grateful tears and he scampered off as if he was worried Andrea was going to change her mind.

"How much did you give him?" Bethany asked as they jumped into the vehicle.

"I only gave him five dollars but that's as good as a hundred-dollar bill around here," she murmured back. Again, Bethany was overcome with sadness.

Dr. Martinez took the wheel and began to drive out of the airport area. Bethany marveled at how laid back the travellers seemed. It was contrary to anything she had ever seen in the United States. No one seemed to be in a rush to go anywhere. As if reading her thoughts, Dr. Martinez spoke.

"Our way of life is quite a bit different than that you are accustomed," he told her. "Nicaragua is the second poorest country in the western hemisphere. Our major exports are coffee, tobacco, sugar and gold but of course those products are very weather and climate dependant. Tourism has increased in the past decade so we are told our economy is on the rise however, there is still much disease and a need for clean water."

Bethany leaned forward between the front seats to absorb every word.

"I thought that there were many fresh water lakes in this country," Bethany piped up and Dr. Martinez nodded.

"That is true but they are mostly infested with bacteria. We simply don't have the resources to filter the water. Most people drink from the lakes and end up with E-coli, parasites and in the case of Dario's sister, Luz, cholera."

Bethany was aghast.

"We have to do something about that!" she cried passionately and both Andrea and the doctor chuckled gently.

"There simply is not the money," he said sadly. "But God sends us angels like you to make things easier sometimes."

They were silent for the remainder of the trip, Bethany lost in thought as the lush but impoverished setting slipped before her wide eyes.

They don't have clean water and they get sick from it. If they don't have money for clean water, they definitely don't have money for the medicine to cure them of the illnesses. It makes more sense for them to spend the money on the water than it does to pay for the aftermath of drinking tainted liquid. But if there is no money, how do we make this happen?

Bethany had no answer.

When they arrived at their hotel, Bethany was immediately repulsed. The three-story building was crumbling from the inside out. Their room was miniscule and stifling hot.

"Where is the bathroom?" she asked Andrea, dropping her case reluctantly onto the floor beside one of the twin beds.

"It's a common bathroom down the hall," she replied, plopping heavily onto the bed. A huge insect scurried out from its hiding spot, causing Bethany to scream. Andrea laughed.

"You better get used to the bugs," she teased. "There are creatures you can't imagine in these parts. And lizards as big as your head."

Bethany shuddered, eyeing the scuttling insect. She closed her eyes and took a deep breath.

I can do this for thirteen more days, she told herself. *Just focus on the sick kids and forget about the twenty-six-legged animal under your bed.*

Bethany was sure she wouldn't sleep for the remainder of the trip.

"Get changed. We have to get to the clinic," Andrea pressed. "We have to meet the others soon."

Bethany nodded and headed into the hallway to find the washroom. The plumbing was ancient and everything leaked from the sink to the toilet. The shower consisted of a drain over a set of floor tiles and a long hose.

I wonder if this water is safe for showering.

She wet a washcloth and wiped her face carefully, avoiding her orifices lest the water was contaminated. She would have to ask Andrea about it.

Or I can ask the doctor, Bethany thought, her mind recalling the wisdom and depth of his brown eyes. *I bet he knows everything.*

Bethany returned to the room and slipped into a simple white sundress.

"What do we do at the clinic?" she asked, waiting for Andrea to get ready.

"We will devise a plan. Half of us will go to the church for the first week and supply the children with books, pencils, papers and other necessities for school. We'll do activities with the kids, just as we do at home in Sunday school. The second week, we will switch and stay at the clinic helping the doctors with the sick. Dr. Martinez will show you what needs to be done there. We'll figure out which group you and I will fall into when we meet the others today."

Bethany was surprised to find herself hoping she was on clinic duty.

I am interested to see how medicine is handled in the third world, she told herself but she knew she was lying. She wanted to spend more time with the attractive doctor. She had only spent moments with Dr. Martinez but she found him intriguing. His work was thankless and never ending yet he maintained an almost cheerful aura as if he was unaffected by the endless suffering in which he was surrounded.

Andrea turned to her and waved a chubby hand.

"I'm ready, Beth. Let's go – the car will be waiting."

When they arrived at the Managua Children's Clinic, Bethany was taken aback. The air of serenity which had floated over Managua, shadowing them from the airport had evaporated. In its place was havoc. In every corner of the tiny building lay children in various stages of agony. Some were vomiting on the floor, others were clinging to their defeated looking mothers. The stench of disease and urine wafted into her nose but Bethany was too wrapped up in the mollifying sights to notice the putrid stench. While a few small beings were lucky enough to have claimed beds, the majority were laying on the floor. Almost all of them were crying. Bethany fought back her own tears, springing into action.

"What can I do?" she cried to Andrea. To her surprise, the older woman stood back, her mouth turned down in grief.

"Just wait. The doctor will tell us what to do," she replied but Bethany could barely hear her above the din.

"We just can't stand here!" Bethany insisted. "We have to do something!"

Andrea shook her head and her shoulders sagged.

"It is always like this," she replied, anguish in her voice. "All we can do is wait for Dr. Martinez to tell us what to do or else we may be more of a hindrance than a help."

As if on cue, the doctor hurried up to them.

"Ah wonderful! You have arrived. How is your hotel?" Bethany stared at him in disbelief.

How can he ask about our hotel when these children are in such pain?

But as she had the thought, she quickly realized he was simply trying to put them at ease.

"Fine," she replied shortly. "What can I do here?"

Nodding approvingly at her eagerness to get started, he handed her a pair of scrubs and another pair to Andrea.

"After you have put these on, go around to all of the children and try to have them drink a few sips of water. Do not give them too much or they will vomit and it will not only be counterproductive, it will be a waste of good water. There are cases of bottled water which your group brought in my office yesterday. I have the key and you will need to come to me for it every time you need more bottles. I have the only copy. It is important that you keep whatever bottles you have on you at all times or they will be stolen."

Bethany stared at him in shock.

"Who will steal bottles of water from sick children?" she choked in disbelief. Dr. Martinez shrugged as if the information was commonplace.

"These are desperate times, Betany. The children you see here are merely the tip of the iceberg. There are many who live too far away to come here for medical attention. Their families are just as desperate to see them well as the families you see here."

Bethany paled, thinking of impoverished children laying untreated in remote areas of the country, waiting for certain death.

"What happens to them? They are just left to die?" Bethany demanded, gulping at the thought. Dr. Martinez shook his head and smiled.

"No, of course not. I will go to the rural areas three times a week after I leave the clinic to tend to those children also. Luz, Dario's sister is one of my out patients. If I get word of a sick child, I attend to them right away but oftentimes, I am not notified until it is much too late."

Bethany was overcome with emotions so strong, she was almost brought to her knees.

When does this man sleep? He works all day and then travels around at night to do the same, horrific work.

He seemed to read her mournful expression and offered her another kind smile.

"Sometimes they get well," he told her, handing her the key. "We must focus on the positive because that is all we have." She nodded and snapped to attention, hurrying toward the office. She threw on the scrubs and armed herself with several bottles of water which she found piled in a corner.

There are not nearly enough bottles here, she thought, looking hopelessly at the cases. She returned to the exterior of the clinic and knelt next to the nearest child.

"Hi, honey," she whispered to the little girl of about two. The child stared up at her with hollow, hurting eyes and Bethany fought the urge to sob.

"Have some water," she offered, pressing the bottle to her parched lips. The baby tried to struggle against her but Bethany held her firmly and managed to get a few drops of water into her.

"Rest now," she whispered, stroking her tiny face. As if she understood, her lids closed heavily. Bethany moved on to the next child and, sweetly feeding him the clean liquid.

Bethany had been at it for over an hour, oblivious to everything but the little bodies in her care when someone tapped her shoulder. Slightly annoyed at the distraction, Bethany peered up and found herself staring into Dr. Martinez's deep eyes. Her irritation dissolving, she rose to her feet.

"I'm sorry to interrupt you, Miss Betany," he told her, his thick Spanish accent still unable to handle the "h" in her name. "But you forgot to return the key to me."

Apologetically, Bethany reached into the small pocket in her scrubs to retrieve the office key.

"I'm sorry," she told him, handing it back to him. "I am just on my way over there now anyway. I need more water."

Dr. Martinez looked around appreciatively.

"You managed to get a lot of them to drink," he remarked. "That is no easy feat. Most are feeling so ill, they will not accept anything orally."

Bethany lowered her head humbly.

"They did not fuss very much," she told him. "I fear they are too sick to argue."

The two turned back to the office and Dr. Martinez unlocked the door to allow them to enter.

"Dr. Martinez – "

He faced her abruptly.

"Please call me Jasiel," he told her. Bethany felt a small fission of pleasure course through her as he said his name. His fixed his penetrating eyes upon her and she felt her cheeks stain pink under his gaze.

"Jasiel," she continued, trying to force the blush from her cheeks. "Where do you get aid from if things are so dire in your country?"

He pursed his lips together as he dug through the drawers looking for something.

"Mostly we depend on emergency relief from other countries. The United States in a big provider in assistance. The biggest problem we face, unfortunately, is that we simply do not have enough medical staff to deal with the sick."

Bethany busied herself collecting more bottles, her mind racing with thoughts.

We will have to do something about this.

The week seemed to fly by, the days blurring together one after the other. There was no time to explore the ancient and mystic city of Managua as the group worked tirelessly from sun up to sun down at the clinic. Even though she was in the company of her fellow church friends, Bethany barely saw them except briefly in the mornings and evenings at meals. When they finally made it back to the hotel, they inhaled supper and generally fell into a deep, exhaustive slumber. Bethany's concern that she would be unable to sleep with the critters with whom she was rooming proved unfruitful. The lizards had begun to grow on her with their nonchalant expressions and beady little eyes.

The only constant that Bethany had was Jasiel who seemed to take special interest in helping her adjust. He allowed her to perform basic medical procedures, despite her protests.

"I have no training!" she had cried the first time he handed her a needle. The handsome doctor had shaken his head wryly, pressing the instrument into her hand.

"Then you are still more qualified than most of the people whom we have here," he replied. Gulping, Bethany had accepted and under his careful guidance, she began administering much needed medicine to the children.

On the fourth day, little Lilliam rose to her feet and walked for the first time. She had been in the clinic for two weeks, unable to move.

"Jasiel!" Bethany screeched. "Lilliam is walking!"

He had nodded stoically but his face registered relief.

"Thank God," he whispered. "I was beginning to lose faith in her chances for survival."

Bethany impulsively embraced him in a hug before attending to the child. She did not see the look of longing gave to her disappearing back.

Later that evening as they began to close the clinic, Jasiel took her aside and out of earshot of Andrea and Jack who were stripping the linens from the beds.

"It was because of you that Lilliam finally was able to move from bed," he told her solemnly. Pleased but unwilling to take the credit, Bethany shook her head.

"No, it was God's hand at work here," she told him.

"Yes, it was God who sent you to us but it was your attention to that child which made her well again. If we had only a few more people to spend the time with these babies..."

Bethany did not know how to respond. She looked into his eyes, wanting desperately to end his suffering as much as he wished to end that of the children. He gave her a weak smile and again, Bethany was affected by a shiver.

Over and above his tireless efforts, he must be very lonely. He spends most of his time alone or surrounded by children. I wonder how his wife feels about him being gone so often.

Bethany decided to ask.

"How does your wife handle your hours?" she blurted out. He raised an eyebrow in surprise.

"I am not married. No woman in her sane mind would stand for the type of work I have committed myself to." He paused and looked at Bethany thoughtfully. "I thought you would have figured out that I was unmarried by now."

A rush of heat colored Bethany's cheeks under his wistful stare. She dropped her head in embarrassment.

He feels it too, she thought, her heart pounding in her chest. *We have a connection but it can never be...can it?*

"Beth! Dr. Martinez is here!" Andrea called from the doorway later that evening. Bethany almost tripped over her feet in her rush to the threshold. Andrea tried to step out of her way but the size of the room made the dance almost impossible. Eventually, Andrea ended up behind the flimsy wooden door. Jasiel stood in the hallway appearing exhausted.

"Jasiel, what are you doing here?" she asked, shooting Andrea a covert glance. The woman raised her eyebrow questioningly.

"Jasiel?" she mouthed silently, trapped in her spot but Bethany ignored her.

"I hope you will forgive the intrusion, Betany," he said. "But I am about to head into the rural areas. I thought you might wish to join me and meet some of the children outside of the city."

Eagerly, Bethany nodded. She had been wondering about the children outside the city. Her plan had been to ask to accompany him later in the week but it seemed that he had read her mind.

"I would love to!" she exclaimed and Jasiel nodded happily. "I'll be back later, Andy."

Andrea shrugged her shoulders and collapsed on the bed.

"I'll likely be sound asleep," she replied, already closing her eyes.

The drive from Managua to Masaya took forty-five minutes in Jasiel's old van and it was the first time Bethany had an opportunity to see the incredible Nicaraguan countryside. Bethany's breath was stolen by the towering palms and the untouched landscape.

"This is what the dinosaurs saw!" Bethany proclaimed, staring open-mouthed at the mountains against the glorious sunset. Jasiel chuckled.

"Yes, we do not have much industry in Nicaragua," he agreed.

As night began to fall, the smooth fields became a sprinkling of dilapidated shanties and Jasiel pulled his car to a stop. A sudden fear seized Bethany as people began to poke their heads from the depth of the seemingly abandoned properties.

"There are people in there," she whispered as Jasiel collected supplies. He glanced at her, realizing she was serious.

"Yes, Betany. This is where people live," he told her.

Just when I thought I could not be any more shocked by the living conditions in this country, Bethany thought, gritting her teeth. She quickly began to assist the doctor and followed him up to a tin shack. Immediately, the door flew open and Dario stood, his eyes red from crying. He began to babble in Spanish and was joined by an older woman. The two barraged Jasiel with words which Bethany could not understand but she recognized the urgency in their tone.

"What happened?" she whispered, almost running after Jasiel into the house. He did not need to answer. Laying on a pallet on the floor was a small girl in the throes of eternal sleep. A hand flew to Bethany's mouth as she gasped back a sob. It was Dario's sister, Luz.

The doctor leaned forward to check for signs of life but there were none. Luz was gone.

Bethany wanted to scream, to cry out and yell at God but she did none of those things. This was not about her deep regret. Dario and his mother had lost a small, precious soul and their anguish was fresh and real. Immediately, Bethany reached out to embrace Dario who clung to her like a burr. She whispered calmingly into his ear as he cried, his frail body trembling in shock.

Jasiel scooped up Luz's lifeless body and walked her to the van while Bethany stroked Dario's hair. When he returned, he spoke to the family in low tones and nodded at Bethany to follow him.

"We must return to Managua to arrange for Luz's body to be cremated," Jasiel told her. "The family has no means to provide for a proper burial."

His voice was raw with grief. Bethany slowly reclaimed her seat on the passenger's side of the car and lowered her gaze so she would not see Luz's mother chasing after the van, calling out for her daughter.

On the sixth day, it was time for the group to switch. Bethany was supposed to join Andrea and Jack at the church but as she reluctantly geared up for the switch that morning at the hotel, there was a knock at the door.

Aimee Thompson, the mission co-ordinator wanted to speak with Bethany.

"There's been a change of plans if it's okay with you," Aimee told her. Bethany stared at her quizzically.

"Dr. Martinez has requested that you stay at the clinic for the remainder of the trip. He says that the children have become very attached to you and honestly, it's not fair to upset them any more than they've already been upset. Is that something you can live with?" Aimee asked. Bethany nodded with too much enthusiasm.

"Oh, yes ma'am!" she declared. "I can definitely stay at the clinic for the rest of the trip!"

As Aimee left, Andrea shot Bethany a sly smile.

"I'm sure it's only for the good of the children," Andrea joked. "It has nothing to do with the handsome, attentive doctor who seems to stare at you everywhere you go."

"Of course it's for the children!" Bethany retorted angrily. "What a horrible suggestion that I am using sick kids for a romantic interest."

Andrea lost the smile and shook her head.

"I would never say that. I know your heart and intentions are true, Beth. I would also have to be deaf, blind and dumb not to see the way you and Dr. Martinez have connected...or can I call him Jasiel also?"

Bethany grimaced. Luz's death had a much bigger impact on her than she had expected, affecting her mood substantially. She had thrown herself completely into the care of the children, staying well after the others had gone back to the hotel for the night. She and Jasiel had become joined at the hip and while Luz had been the one that got away, other boys and girls seemed to be thriving in the short time since she had arrived.

"Well, I hope you don't become too attached, Beth. You're going to be heartbroken when it's time to go home," Andrea commented casually. Bethany felt the blood drain from her face. She had purposely avoided thinking about the impending departure but Andrea's words had forced the unwanted thoughts into mind.

What will I do when it is time to leave?

On the last night the group was to be in Nicaragua, Jasiel appeared at the hotel again. This time Bethany answered the door. Her heart was an explosion of bittersweet emotion as she stared into his soulful eyes.

"Would do you do me the honor of having dinner with me this evening?" he asked her. Not trusting her voice, Bethany nodded and allowed for Jasiel to lead her into the city. He had arranged for a romantic table inside a small, cozy restaurant.

As soon as they were seated, he grasped her hands.

"Betany, I want you to know that these last two weeks have been the best since I began my medical career. I have never been so in tune with anyone or met another person who seemed to care about the children as much as I do."

Bethany forced a lump down her windpipe and willed herself not to cry.

"I know we are worlds apart but I wanted to let you know how I feel before you leave. I hope you will consider coming back on another trip."

Bethany blinked the tears from her eyes.

"What has happened here has exceeded my wildest imagination," she told him seriously, squeezing his palms. "I have never felt more enlightened or awake..."

Or in love, she added silently. They shared a melancholic smile and forced themselves to concentrate on their last moments together, pushing the impending unhappiness of tomorrow from their minds.

"That was a lovely trip," Andrea commented, as the plane began to taxi down the runway. She nodded absently, staring toward the airport.

"I think that we are making some progress here, though, don't you?" Andrea asked. Her question went unanswered and she sighed heavily.

"Hello? Are you ignoring me for any particular reason?"

She turned to face Andrea and smiled sheepishly.

"Sorry. I am just wondering if we made the right decision allowing Bethany to stay behind," Aimee replied. Andrea laughed.

"I don't think we had much of a choice," Andrea replied. "Short of dragging her on the plane, she was staying."

Aimee nodded absently, a sweet smile touching her lips. She raised her eyes toward the ceiling of the aircraft and winked.

"You know what you're doing up there," she told the heavens.

WHEN ANGELS LISTEN

79

BONNIE WILLIAMS

The man in front of her looked worse every day. Henry Whitwood was a man in his fifties, but he had always seemed like a strapping youngster to Vera with his endless supply of vigor. That was before he caught something nasty. It had only been a few days ago that he started looking weak, and by now he already looked ready to fall over.

Vera tried to help by making him some soothing herbal tea. However, with Henry's illness also came a serious loss of appetite. The man hadn't touched food since he picked Vera up from the Romanov-on-Murman port. Right now he was even unable to stand. He sat down on a closed barrel of wine, looking out at sea with a pained expression on his face. Vera sat on the floor, her long black skirt fluttering in the wind despite her attempts to keep it still. Her hair received similar abuse thanks to the rough sea. She would have bristled yarn for hair by the time they reached America.

She was afraid that making any noise would make his headache worse. So she just silently looked out at sea, smelling the salty air all around her. Minutes ticked by with each breath, and Vera counted each one. She could be sewing a new dress right about now, but her concern for her friend took away all her attention.

"How's your head fairing?" she asked in her thick accent.

For a long while she received no response. He must've fallen asleep. She pulled out a piece of parchment from the folds of her dress and began to read. The sender told her of great tales about cowboys fighting the natives, the hot sun that shone all year long, and the bright yellow corn that bore fruit in the summer. In return she told him what her country was like. He responded that he would like to see it one day. This was just one of many, many letters he written to her.

Both Vera Zykov and Liam Whitwood both suffered from lack of family. Both had a love of learning about the world. Both had a desire to find their soul mate. They were like two missing puzzle pieces that found each other over seas. That was why Vera was on this boat right now, following Liam's uncle to America.

The old man stirred, "Did you say something, dear?"

"I asked how you were feeling."

"Better, I think," the man winced, "Then again, maybe not."

"You shouldn't push yourself, sir. Your illness will only get worse if you do."

"I'm fine, Bepa," he laughed at their little inside joke. When signing onboard, Vera had accidentally spelled half her name in Cyrillic. The man who read it out loud pronounced it like an American, with R as P and V as B. Vera had been embarrassed at first. However, her friend's laughter soon became contagious, until even she cracked a smile at the nickname.

Vera decided to change the topic.

"Mr. Whitwood. Why didn't you let Liam on board? He told me in his letter that he wanted to be the one to see me."

Henry slowly tilted his head toward her, the shadows etching along his laugh lines made him look like a portrait than a real human being. His skin had become so sickly that it almost looked to her like paint.

"Because I have all the experience as a sailor. And he has all the youth. I told him...I said he needed to stay at the farm so that we had food when we got back. He wasn't happy. No siree. But he knew that I had a point."

Vera fell silent, causing Henry to give her a curious look.

"Is something on your mind?"

"Huh? Oh no, sir." In all honesty, she had a lot on her mind. What if there was no Liam Whitwood? Or what if he was already married?

What if he was nothing like his letters described?

Vera knew it was foolish to question herself now. She was already out at sea, well on her way to another country that she had never been to before. She knew going in how much of a gamble she was taking by following Henry.

It was either take a gamble in order to marry for love, or stay where she would be doomed to marry someone she didn't. She knew that she could love no one in her town as well as she loved the man in her letters. Something about how Liam wrote showed sincerity and kindness. Truly that wasn't something a fake man could fabricate.

.....Right?

They watched the sun as his set on the horizon, shading in the sky with golds and purples. Vera sat by Henry's side as they took this journey together.

Days passed with Vera witnessing things she could only have dreamed about before. They got off the port and took a horse to Virginia. She saw what they meant by the wild west. Unlike her city that was filled with people and frost, this place was filled with sand and wide open spaces. They would be on the horse for an entire day without coming across a single other person.

Henry ate, but only from Vera's prodding. He regained a little bit of strength. Finally, they arrived to the Virginian town known as Sungale.

Sungale was barely a few years old as an established location, and Vera could quickly see that. They had only come across a few buildings that seemed miles apart from each other. According to Henry, this spot used to be reserved for hunting, which was why it had remained untouched as a town for so long. In the end, it seemed that the Americans decided they needed more places to live.

Looking at it, Vera was awed by how close to nature this little town was. It was like something out of one of her fairytale books that she had when she was younger: long, yellow wheat, cows and bison wandering the earth, and a dirt road that was barely paved by human hands.

The dust itched at her nose, causing her eyes to water. She managed to avoid sneezing. Henry, on the other hand, didn't fare nearly as well. As soon as they got into town, he began coughing a lung out.

"You must be sick," Vera said.

"Nothing a little time won't cure," he stated between gasps, "Thank you for your concern."

He meant that to be the end of the discussion. Vera reluctantly let it slide, even though her worry grew.

Finally, they happened upon a small wooden house that would just barely house three people. Despite its size, Vera loved it immediately. Its humbleness matched the surrounding area. And it wasn't as though there hadn't been any effort put in to making it look like a house. The roof had been outlined with blue paint that matched the sky. The windows looked brand new. But what most charmed Vera was the small door that had the same color as the roof's exterior. It also had a knob that was painted golden yellow in a way that reminded Vera of the wheat fields.

She found herself enchanted. Despite how tired her bones were from the long distance traveling, she hurried off the horse and led it to the watering hole, where it gave itself a much deserved drink. Henry steadily got off after her, not in his usual energetic way when he would deliver letters to her, but in a slow, pained way.

He motioned for her to follow him. Her heart drummed as they entered the house. A man in his early twenties sat in the living room, polishing a hunting rifle. He took one look at her and stopped what he was doing. Gulping, Vera just inspected him in silence.

At least he looked just as his letters described. Black hair, grey eyes, a little lanky for someone of his occupation, and tiny freckles across his tanned cheeks. A cowboy hat sat right beside him on the table.

The man stood up as soon as they entered. He looked at Vera, who could only stare back. What did you say to a man you're engaged to, and you've only just met?

"Um...hello," she greeted uncertainly.

Liam took a hold of her hand and placed it against her lips. In their letters they spoke of how they enjoyed reading about castles, kings, love and war. Vera immediately knew that this was his way to make her feel welcomed. Her lips spread into a soft smile. He stared up at her.

"It's very nice to finally see you in person."

"Then you really are Liam."

"Yes. And you're no doubt Vera."

"How are you so sure?"

"You're exactly as your letters described. And I knew when writing to you that I was speaking to someone honest."

"Thank you," Vera smiled, feeling partially relieved and partially awkward. This was going to take some time to get adjusted to. Even for things like love, results didn't usually happen overnight.

"How are you feeling, Uncle Henry?" Liam turned to the old man. Henry crouched down on the chair and sighed.

"Just a little tired from the trip."

"You sure? You're looking pale."

"I told him that he needed some rest," Vera pointed out to her finance.

Henry, realizing that he was just about to get tag teamed, immediately changed the topic. He motioned toward his left.

"I see you finished her gift."

He was pointing at a rocking chair that Vera didn't notice before. Now that she got a better look, she noticed the intricate feminine details that stated this seat was for a woman. Flower designs went in curls across the polished wood.

"I was so excited about meeting you that I made you a chair. Though I should've waited until you got here. I didn't realize how small you were," Liam admitted, sounding ashamed.

It was true that Vera was almost a mouse compared to these two men in the room. And although the chair was closer to her size than theirs, it was still a little big. In all honesty, Vera was the smallest woman of her age back in Russia.

"Thank you, Liam. I love it."

The two looked at each other for a long while. However, the silence wasn't that tense. The longer she studied Liam, the more relaxed she became. Now that she knew that he was real and exactly as he said he was, she felt much better about her decision.

Vera and Henry spent the rest of the day recovering from their long trip. By morning, Vera was already making breakfast and Liam was out watering the crops. He didn't return until late morning, and Henry still hadn't gotten out of bed. Vera was setting the table when she noticed this.

"You don't suppose that his illness has gotten worse?"

Liam tried to smile reassuringly, but she could sense a trace of concern drifting through his eyes.

"Let me see if I can wake him up. I'll be right back."

Vera had already got everything on the table by the time she realized that Liam had not returned. A sinking feeling sprouted inside her chest. She made a move to head down the hallway, but stopped when she saw Liam approaching. His smile was more convincing this time around.

"I think his old age has made him more tired. He wouldn't wake up no matter how much I tried. I figured I would just let him sleep 'til he woke."

Vera nodded. She masked her concern with a pleasant smile, just like she was taught to do in Russia. Husbands wanted happy working wives, no matter how bleak the situation might seem.

Despite her efforts, it seemed that Liam caught onto her worry. He proposed that they go into town after breakfast.

"But what about your uncle?" she couldn't help but ask.

"Uncle Henry's always been tough as nails. I doubt a little cold will keep him bedridden for long."

But what if it's not a cold?

Vera kept her thoughts to herself. The last thing she wanted to do was cause him more concern than necessary.

"Alright. If you're sure that he'll be fine by himself. What do you need in town?"

"I wanted to introduce you," Liam said, "It can get lonely here in this little farm. And you told me how much you love company. I wanted to see if you can find some friends."

"That's very kind of you. But I have you now....don't I?" she averted her gaze. Why was she still worried about this? Why did she still have doubts that this path of love would lead to her happiness? Hadn't she felt it in her heart that this was the right choice?

He took her hand into his. It was almost twice the size of hers. Liam wasn't what she would call a big man, however. Vera realized how small she really was.

She looked up at her fiancé's eyes. His pink lips spread into a kind smile, his blue eyes glistening with pleasure. It was as if simply looking at her brought him great joy. Vera couldn't help but smile back.

"You will always have me. Like I said in the letters, I know how much you're sacrificing to come here."

"You're sacrificing a lot too," she pointed out, "You told me that you left your home to be in this farm."

"That's true. But I have Uncle Henry. You only just got here. I don't want you to feel like you're alone. And I know some women in town that like to talk with each other a lot. So I figured...." he trailed off. Vera finished his thought for him.

"I understand. I think it's a splendid idea having some female friends. Do you get along with the men in town?"

"Most of them," Liam smiled, "They're all the same as me. Guys who work with their hands. You won't find too many rich folk here, as this town is mostly people starting all over with their lives. Making new buildings, plowing new fields....it's not as easy as some people dream about."

"Maybe that's why it's so romantic. All the hard work one person can do," Vera said more to herself than to her fiancé.

They rode the farm's horse into town. Vera pressed herself against Liam's back, the summer sun making her sleepy. It would take her a while to get used to this heat.

Sungale looked more like a marketplace than the entire town. The bank, sheriff's office, library, school and shops were all in this one small area. Their horse suddenly found a certain spot of grass that must've been different from the others, for it stopped to have itself a snack.

Liam got off and helped Vera down as well, gently placing her feet on the soft ground. A few people approached them with curious looks on their faces.

"Who we got here, Liam?" a man asked.

"Is she new here?" a woman asked another woman.

Someone turned to Liam with a knowing eye.

"I see you found your soul mate."

Vera paused at those sudden choice of words. True, she did believe Liam was meant to be with her. But how did this man know that?

Liam wrapped his arms around her.

"You're right, Orwell. This is Vera, everybody. We've been writing to each other for a few years."

"Vera?" one of the woman turned up her nose and scoffed, "That doesn't sound very American. Where is she from? Why Liam....there are plenty of good girls within the same country as you. You don't need to go shopping for a bride."

Vera's face warmed with shame. Liam came to her defense.

"She may not be American, Scarlett. But she's one in a million. I doubt that I'd be able to find anybody like her in this country."

Now Vera's cheeks were warm with pleasure. She didn't need any more proof now. This man was everything he was in his letters: courageous, hardworking, and had a way with words. Even Scarlett didn't have a retort for that.

Orwell touched Liam's shoulder.

"Glad you're here. We could use some help getting Earl's cows together. He'll pay us, right Earl?"

They turned to a man with the expression of a lost lamb.

"Um....I'll give you dinner. Is that okay, Orwell?"

The gang laughed, clearly not expecting money in the first place. Vera was awed by their love to help one another. No wonder cowboys could do so much. God smiled on them for their selflessness. For you shall never see a brother's ox fall down and ignore him. How rare it was to see that scripture actually taken to heart.

The girls suddenly got excited. One person grabbed Vera's arm and led her to where they were going to watch. Liam smiled at her. It seemed that she was already making friends.

"What are they doing?" Vera asked the woman whose name she'll later learn as Mary.

"See all the cows around here? The cowboys are going to get them back into that pin over there. They finished grazing, so they need to make sure they don't escape now."

Vera looked to where all the men got on horses. Her Liam had been supplied with a younger, more energetic colt than the one they rode to town on. The horse whinnied in excitement, ready to start sprinting in whatever direction Liam chose.

The men lined up. Orwell issued his order.

"Whoever herds the most wins a drink. Wilder over there's keeping score," he pointed to a teenager with a notepad and a cowboy hat, "Go!"

The girls and Vera watched as the men turned their work into a game. Their horses rushed toward the cows, causing them to sprint away. One cowboy threw a rope that latched onto a horn, throwing the bull right on the ground. The cowboy jumped off his horse in order to tie down the cow's legs.

This was the first time that Vera witnessed real cowboys herding cattle. Her eyes widened in awe at the amazing sight. Something far beyond her imagination could grasp.

She smiled when she saw how Liam already gotten three cows into the pen. He laughed with all the other cowboys, looking like the book definition of merry.

Then something horrifying happened. A rather large bull knocked itself against Orwell's horse. The impact sent the man flying toward the ground. Vera screamed when he landed right on top of his head!

"Goodness, is he okay?" Mary asked. The men had already gathered around Orwell, hiding his body from sight.

No, he wasn't okay, Vera decided. No one could recover from that sort of head trauma. Liam pushed his way through the crowd to check on him. Vera mentally prepared to hear how Orwell was either dead or severely damaged.

To her shock, Liam and Orwell came into view, Orwell looking little more than dazed. There was no hint that anything was broken. The men and women all hurled around them. Vera kept a close eye on the man her fiancé was holding onto.

"Is he alright?" someone from the crowd asked.

"Got the reflexes of a cat," Orwell answered with pride, "I landed feet first on the ground. That helped broke my fall. But now I think I need to sit down for a while."

"You're right. I'll help you. Mary. Vera. Can you two go into Earl's house and fetch some water?" Liam asked.

"I'll help too. We can all make some coffee and cakes," Scarlett announced, ready to please Liam. It got on Vera's nerves.

The gaggle of women went inside the house. It appeared as though Earl would have to buy dinner, since they ended using his ingredients. Vera had little doubt that her fiance would pay the man back.

"You must be really worried," Mary pointed out from behind Vera. She noticed that the Russian woman had been keeping a close eye on Orwell. In truth, Vera had a bad feeling about him. Despite what he said, she knew what she saw. He had landed on his head. He should either be dead or unconscious right now.

Vera took the warnings of the Good Book to heart. She knew there was such a thing as unholy spirits. And she knew they could disguise themselves inside human flesh. But fewer and fewer people believed in such a thing anymore. It would do no good to warn Liam and the others of her suspicions.

She decided to let God help her, remembering what she learned in church. "And he said to them, 'This kind cannot be driven out by anything but prayer.'"

She didn't want to let Mary in on her thoughts.

"You're right. I was shocked to see him stand up after that. Did they catch the bull?"

"Your Liam did. He was always good with animals. Not so much with his crops. When he was a child, he didn't water the wheat enough in the summertime. It nearly caused them to burst in flames. He got into so much trouble. I don't think he ever got the knack for that."

Vera remembered all the produce that their own farm had. Mary's words gave her a sinking feeling. She made a mental note to check on the crops occasionally.

"Dear. Can you bring me some water?" Orwell asked Vera.

The woman froze up on the spot. If Orwell was unnerved by her reaction, he didn't show it. Mary gave her a strange look before grabbing a glass of water herself and bringing it to him.

Vera walked outside. She had just arrived in town and already she was screwing up. Maybe Orwell wasn't a demon. Maybe she had only imagined the injury.

"Bepa?" Liam's voice asked.

Vera stiffened. She faced her fiancé with wide eyes.

"How...?"

"How did I know about that nickname?" Liam chuckled, "Uncle Henry told me in his letters."

Vera averted her gaze. She was still ashamed of herself for the Orwell incident, and now she was embarrassed by the story. Liam took hold of her hand with a soft smile on his face. She smiled back.

"I think it's cute. I'd love to call you that, if that's alright with you."

Vera hugged him, "You may call me whatever you'd like. I'm yours."

"And I'm yours," he whispered inside her ear, "Bepa."

The marriage was beautiful, the reception grand, and the aftermath a happy ending. Months flew by like seconds. Vera was the happiest woman in the world. Her Liam was everything he said he was and more. To her pleasure, it seemed as though he was really trying to learn from his past mistakes with the crops. He would water them at least three times a day, which was especially draining in this intense heat. She made sure to keep him hydrated by bringing him a picture of water whenever he was out in the field. Sweating profusely, the man would always down the entire picture at an impressive speed.

But the good times came to a screeching halt. Henry's illness only gotten worse. They pretty much establish that he had caught yellow fever. He was bedridden since the wedding, and everyday a little more strength left him. Vera held a glass of water to his lips, daintily tilting it down his throat. Liam entered the room, tired from the long hours of work.

"How you doing, ol'timer?"

Henry opened his mouth, but no sound came out.

"I think he lost his voice. He also seems dazed. I don't think he recognizes me."

Liam offers her a comforting smile. It's a lot more forced than usual, "That's probably not true, right uncle? You know Bepa."

His uncle looked at her, or rather, through her. His eyes had some sort of hazy film over them, as if he couldn't process what's going on.

Vera couldn't take that empty stare. She excused herself and made a hasty retreat. She didn't think she could stand to see that look again.

It turned out she didn't have to. Henry died overnight.

At the funeral, Orwell and the others came to pay their respects. Liam held a solemn gaze. The way he looked at the casket unnerved Vera. Something about that expression did not belong to a strong cowboy. It was a lost look. A weak look.

A sturdy hand touched her shoulder. Vera almost screamed when she saw who it was. Orwell leaned closer to her face in order to speak in a soft whisper.

"Liam needs you now more than ever. Make sure you stay by his side."

Vera barely processed what he said. All she could do was stare into the eyes of the monster. She didn't let herself relax until he lifted her hand off her shoulder. His intense gaze stared through her soul, calculating and emotionless.

When he left, Mary came up to her. She was one of the few who approached the mail order bride. Most people had hovered around Liam at the wake. Even Scarlett chatted him up as if this was just a normal party.

"He's really sad," Mary observed.

"Of course. He just lost his uncle."

"I think there's more to it than that."

Vera paused, "What do you mean?"

"Well, you know that his uncle was the only family he had left, right?"

Vera was insulted. She was Liam's wife. Didn't she technically count as 'family?'

Mary continued, oblivious to her friend's displeasure with her remark.

"His uncle was the one who practically raised him. His uncle taught him how to be a cowboy. Plus, he was the one who helped Liam moved here. I think Liam feels abandoned."

But I feel abandoned too, thought Vera. Her husband had barely spoken a word to her since his uncle's death. He would go out before breakfast and come back well after sunset. Vera had been occupying a lonely house where Henry died in.

Her heart dropped when she remembered that strange glossy look he gave her. She wished she hadn't been so quick to run away. At least then she would've had a better memory of his last moments. What she wouldn't give to hear her nickname from his lips again.

"Are you going to be okay?" Mary asked.

Vera wasn't sure. She wanted to ask her friend for help. But what could little old Mary do?

The Russian woman nodded. She didn't trust her voice to sound convincing enough. Mary patted her shoulder with a reassuring smile.

"It will be okay. He's in a better place."

Vera wished she had never spoken to Mary. She and Liam had to endure more people telling them that Henry "was in a better place" before they were finally allowed to go home.

As soon as they entered the house, Liam headed for the bedroom.

"Liam..." Vera trailed off. She was unsure how to proceed.

Her husband paused for a second, but didn't stop completely. He didn't look in her direction. And he didn't say a word. His newly gruff nature frightened Vera. This was not the man she married. It felt like she had a stranger in the house.

She wanted to tell him this. She wanted to plead with him to be strong for her just like she would try to be strong for him. But the words refused to come. He just stared right through her for so long it made her scared. Slowly, he turned back and walked away. Vera realized that she was all alone.

The next morning was when it started to fall apart.

"Liam?" she called while cleaning the dishes, "What are those hens making so much noise about? Can you check on them?"

No response. She dropped the plate on the counter and went to the other room. Liam sat in silence, polishing his rifle. She licked her lips nervously.

"Liam?"

He didn't say anything. Didn't even look at her. If his hands weren't moving, she might've thought he had turned into a statue.

"Liam. Please check on the hens. I'll go tend to the crops, alright?" she smiled at her compromise. Her smile faltered when seconds ticked by with no response.

Husbands wanted happy wives. Well, wives wanted happy husbands. Or at least husbands that would speak to their wives. Vera couldn't stand to look at him right now. She stomped outside and headed straight for the chicken coop.

Feathers and eggs were everywhere. Liam was the one who cleaned up the chicken coop and fed the hens. Vera noticed that there was no trace of bird feed in the coop. The chickens hollered at her for food, a few pecking her skirt angrily.

She closed her eyes and sighed. The woman went to the tool shed in order to do the chores her husband was supposed to do this morning. She grabbed the large bag of feed, making sure to lift with her knees in order to support it. They kept a ton of it in stock. This was why it was usually up to Liam to do it. Vera wanted nothing more than to go back to cleaning. At least that was work she was used to.

But if no one fed the chickens, their farm wouldn't get eggs, which was its main source of income. She barely made it through the door when a brainless hen got right under her legs, causing her to trip. She yelped. Feed spilled all over her, and the chickens rushed at the food. She sobbed dryly. Here she was, covered in feed, dirt and chickens, while her husband remained worthless.

She threw one bird off her shoulder.

Weeks passed and her husband would barely lift a finger to help her work. Weeks passed and she did both his chores and hers, slept alone because Liam no longer slept, and stopped trying to force food down her husband's throat. Weeks passed and her husband had not said anything to her. Vera had taken up so much work that she could've very well called the farm hers by now.

She carried the heavy sack to the chicken coop. Again she nearly tripped over one of the stupid fowls. She looked at the building. It was so dirty, but she didn't have time to clean it and make food and tend to the crops and feed the animals and churned the butter and sew new clothes for the coming fall.....

She couldn't take it anymore. Rage blinded her to all reason. Before she could consider what she was about to do, Vera stormed back inside.

"You worthless man. I'm ashamed of you."

Liam stopped polishing his rifle. He just stared at her. Vera knew she was being unfair right now. But she was too angry to care. She felt all alone. Without her husband, the only reason she had left her country, she had no one to turn to. It was all too much, and Vera found herself taking all her frustrations out on him.

"Why did I marry you? I was wrong to think that this would work out. I should've stayed in Russia. Now I'm all alone with a man who won't do anything."

Her husband didn't get angry, but his brows creased in sadness. She prayed that was enough to snap him out of it. However, instead of getting off the chair and helping her out, the broken man quietly went back to polishing.

They didn't look at each other for the rest of the evening. That night Vera couldn't sleep. Her dream life had become a nightmare. Every inch of her bones screamed in pain from all the hard labor she endured. And yet now that she had a chance to rest, she couldn't.

Giving up, the Russian went into the living room. Her husband sat snoozing on the chair with his gun in his hands. Vera realized that it was the first time in a long while that she had seen anything except distraught on his face. He almost looked....peaceful.

Vera shook her head. She looked at the chair he had so carefully made her and remembered what he said. He didn't even know how big she was before they decided to get married. Hadn't that been a warning in of itself? They didn't know each other before rushing into marriage. Otherwise she would've known that this would happen after Henry's death.

Letters hadn't been enough, surely.

Vera contemplated what to do now. Could she just leave? Just up and....leave? After all, Liam had obviously decided that she was no longer his priority. And it had been weeks of the same thing over and over again. She couldn't deal with this forever.

Vera sobbed. Maybe it would be better this way. Maybe she could go to Mary's house and ask to stay until she found a way back to Russia. This had all been a terrible mistake.....

She looked at Liam's sleeping face with her heart longing to love him. She refused to listen to it. Look where it got her so far.

Her mind was made up. She would be gone by the time that Liam awoke. Vera went into the barn and saddled the old colt that they had. She made a mental note to figure out a way to give him back to Liam later. The colt looked annoyed that she would make him work this late. She struggled to get on herself since she was so small, but still managed.

She set the horse in motion, dashing off into the night sky with nothing but the full moon as her light. She trusted her memory of the roads because it was so dark. The horse stepped on something wooden, informing her that they just arrived on the bridge.

She stopped. Someone was right in front of her, blocking her path. All she could tell was the manly silhouette. He grabbed onto her horse. She screamed.

"Let go!" she ordered.

"Is that you, Vera?"

The woman's heart continued to drum inside her chest.

"Orwell?" she gasped. She tried not to show her fear. God had not answered her prayers to get rid of this demon. And now it looked as if he had come to seek its vengeance on her.

"Calm down. I just want to talk to you."

"Let go."

She ushered for her horse to get out of there. But the colt remained motionless, almost as if entranced by this man in front of it. The man held up a lantern, revealing his face. Fear took control over everything else.

"I know what you are. Let me go!" she said.

"Please. I want to talk to you about your husband."

"What business is that of yours?"

Then, to her shock, the man let go of the horse. He backed away, but still stood right in the middle of the bridge. He held his arms out like a martyr preparing for his sacrifice.

"If you don't want to talk, I will let you leave. But keep in mind what you're about to do. I will not force you to stay and listen to me, but God is watching."

He spoke with sincerity, and with such adoration when he said God's name that it made Vera pause. Demons feared the Lord so much that they dared not speak His name. So how could he say it with such ease?

Vera got off the horse and slowly approached him. Logic told her to run far away. But something kept her feet moving forward. Maybe it was hope that he could tell her something she needed to hear.

"What is it?" she asked after a long silence.

Orwell's shoulders relaxed.

"I believe fate brought us together. Vera, I want to tell you that you can't leave your husband."

Vera didn't question how he knew what she was doing. Even if she decided he wasn't a demon after all, she still had a feeling that he was inhuman in some way.

He waited for her to respond. She just stood in silence, so he continued.

"Your husband isn't the strongest man alive. And that's why he needs you."

Vera shrank away at the responsibility she had been supplied with. Orwell noted her reluctance with a patient smile.

"He needs you to be his wife."

"You don't understand," she pouted like she was a child. She knew she was being unreasonable. But once again, she was too distraught to care.

"Then tell me until I do understand."

They were words of kindness, not mocking in the slightest. The man continued to hold the lantern up to his head so that she might see the sincerity on his face. She inhaled sharply.

"I'm in love with him...."

"....but?"

"I....I don't know what to do. He's throwing all of his problems on me."

"He's your husband. His problems are now your problems."

"But he's not the man he once was. Am I being cruel? I know his uncle died, but I've lost family too. Why do I have to be strong enough to keep us both together, while he does nothing?"

Right after she said it, she knew how selfish that was. The woman held her breath. She suddenly felt like God was glaring down at her in disappointment.

Orwell took his time coming toward her. He held the lantern on her face, taking in her expression.

His eyes were kind, "Your problems are his too. Tell me. If you love him, why are you running away?"

"....I don't know."

"Is it because you love him that you're leaving? Is it because you're tired of seeing him suffer?"

Shocked, Vera stared in awe at the man in front her. It was as if Orwell read her mind and put them into better words than she could voice herself. She had expected him to be angry with her for trying to leave. Instead he just stared at her with the upmost patience.

Could he be an angel of God?

The woman looked at him again, trying to see if there was some holy light circling around him. But his human disguise was flawless.

"You can still make the right choice. Turn back and go to him. You are one half of your husband's flesh. Without that half he will surely die."

Vera froze up. She hadn't thought about the scripture in that way. She hadn't considered how much Liam needed her. She figured that if she left, Liam would find a way to support himself again.

Had she been wrong?

The woman sobbed as guilt stung her chest. It felt like bees were digging their stingers inside her heart. She barely registered that Orwell had pulled her in for a hug.

"I don't know if I can go back," she admitted.

"Look inside yourself, just like you did when you came to this country. You're a girl who goes with her feelings. It's just that at this point in time, your feelings almost led you astray."

She looked at him with tears falling down her face.

He continued, "You know what the right thing is. God is telling you. I know you love Liam too, so your heart agrees with what God says. So what is telling you to run?"

She paused for a moment, thinking, "Fear."

"Get rid of that fear. God doesn't give anyone a spirit of fear, but of love and self-control."

This man knew his scriptures. He spoke about God like He was the one who personally assigned him this task. Vera looked him in the eye, wondering if it was really true. Did God send one of His angels to stop her?

She decided it must be true.

"Okay. Can you walk me back?"

Liam looked pleased, "Sure."

The minute they arrived at the farm, her husband came toward her. In the lantern light he looked in near hysterics. A flash of relief shone through his eyes, then he glanced at Orwell in suspicion.

"What happened? Where have you guys been, Bepa?" his voice wasn't accusing. But it did sound concern. Such worry touched her heart, making her more ashamed of her actions than ever. Orwell spoke up before she had the chance.

"You were asleep and we were afraid to wake you. I'm afraid I'm responsible for your little scare. I knocked on the door and your wife answered. I needed to borrow a horse to town."

"This late at night?" Liam exclaimed.

"It was an emergency. My own horse gone into labor and we needed to get supplies for a safe delivery. We just finish laying mother and baby to rest, and we're with you now."

Liam suddenly looked guilty.

"You're working at night too?" he sounded distraught, as if he just realized the weight he put on her shoulders.

Vera opened her mouth to say none of it was true. But Orwell looked at her. A flash of insight went through her mine when she looked him in the eye. Liam couldn't take the truth right now.

Liam pulled her into a tight embrace.

"I'm sorry. I should've tried harder. I should've remembered that you lost people too. When I woke up and saw you gone....I snapped out of it. I'm sorry, Bepa. It's just that....Henry was my father."

Tears stung Vera's eyes. She could understand the feeling of losing a parent. She returned the hug, promising herself to never make a repeat of this mistake again.

"I loved him too. But let me grieve with you. Don't push me away anymore."

He leaned his head into hers.

"I promise, Bepa," they kissed. Neither noticed the angel kindly leading the old colt back to the barn for a well-deserved rest. He smiled at the crops that he knew would bear the best fruit in town. God was good.

THE LOVE I LOST

CHAPTER ONE

I always look forward to my early morning jogs.

Only I got a late start today. I didn't arrive at the trail until nearly noon.

A blue sky stretched over the horizon, one of those hot windy days as a strong breeze from the bay blew cool air inland.

I ran past the office park part of the trail, a place that everyone called "the loop." Big windows of the office buildings were tinted blue-purple. Looking ahead, I saw the bridge that connected Bay Farm Island to the Alameda mainland open up and let a small sailboat through. The traffic stacked and honked their horns as the boat made its way through. Rich folks out for a leisurely ride across the bay while making everyone late for work.

I would see the same people on the trail everyday and have sort of an unspoken camaraderie. I would see a red-haired woman in her early sixties that reminded me of my second grade teacher named Mrs. Broussard so I nicknamed her "Missus B" in my mind. I'd say 'good morning' to her each day and on one occasion called her "Missus B."

Oops.

Then I would see a Japanese man who always waved hello while he walked an oversized German Shepherd. I nicknamed him "Mister Miyagi" because he looked like the character in the Karate Kid.

He always had a pleasant smile on his face but I noticed when his dog took a dump he never reached for one of the Mutt Mitts. On two occasions, I saw his dog whom I overheard him call "Tiny" take a apocalyptic size turd on the grass. Then the two would hurry off the trail, both wearing conspiratorial grins as they left their mess behind.

I could only shake my head and laugh.

Until this day. When I stepped right into it.

I felt the squish and nearly pitched backward.

Then I smelled it. The malodorous stink coming hard and fast into my senses.

In the distance, I saw Mr.Miyagi and his dog running away into the fog bank of the San Francisco Bay Area trail.

"Shit!" I called out.

This type of thing is not supposed to happen to people like me. Or so I used to think. I am a teacher with tenure at an affluent Christian school. I can afford to live in a house that is literally a stone's throw away from the bay. I have the use of an easement to the beach (thirty feet wide, no vehicles permitted) and an easement to the trail (twenty feet wide, again don't park your car here please). I am in fantastic shape with no credit card debt or kids. It is my own Great American dream. Enjoy.

Just don't step in shit.

Breathless from my run, I couldn't help but breath in deep. The dog crap made me want to retch. Jesus, what did he feed that thing?

"I'm so sorry," the voice came from behind me.

I turned around and saw him. Slate blue eyes and brown curly hair topped a perfect face. And damn he had some serious biceps showing through on that tight t-shirt.

Biceps which held back a slobbering pit bull.

"Chubbs," he said. "Stop!"

The dog stopped jumping up and down when he saw me but drool came down his mouth. He looked like how I felt.

"There were out of Mutt Mitts," the man said pointing to the dispensary a few feet away. "I had to run over and get some from the next block over. I'm sorry."

I began rubbing my foot on the grass, the crap sliding off, and yeah I'm not usually this sexy.

"You look familiar to me," he said picking up the rest of Chubbs' poo poo with his Mutt Mitt and tossing it in the trash.

I never had a man try and hit on me after I have just stepped in dog shit. I had to laugh.

"No, I don't think we've met."

"Its me, Jennifer. Paul. Paul Demarest."

"No way," I said.

The boy who had a crush on me all the way from seventh grade to high school. The class nerd. The boy that everyone had picked on and made fun of.

He flexed his biceps. "Thirty pounds later and no more bi-focal," he said.

"Yeah, I can see that."

He began to laugh. I couldn't tell if he was laughing at me or with me as I blinked really hard as if my eyes were fooling me. Paul Demarest? The boy everyone called "Poindexter" with derision.

Yep, Poindexter now stood in front of me looking hotter than Brad Pitt ever could.

CHAPTER TWO

"It's pronounced monomial," Paul enunciated the word out. Then laughed as I tried.

"If you are going to make fun of me I'll ask Mr. Hanks to find someone else to tutor me," I said.

"There's no one else. And I don't mean to make fun. I just never heard anyone say it like that. 'Mono-nomial.' I think you just invented a new mathematical classification."

I'll admit, that if pressed, I would have admitted that I did find Paul cute in the eighth grade. But he just didn't register on my spoiled junior high school brat mind. Mr. Hanks, who must have been in his early twenties, stood out as one of my school girl crushes. A fresh college grad whose ears turned red when girls came up and flirted with him.

Yours truly included. I intentionally screwed up on tests so I could be like Tiffany Marie whom he tutored during study hall.

He assigned me to Paul, the resident math whiz and default teacher aide.

"You just have to solve the same problems over and over again," Paul said. "Math is just like anything else. Practice makes perfect. You'll recognize the pattern and figure out the solution"

"I appreciate you helping me," I said. I caressed his arm. To this day, I don't know why.

And he blushed.

"You're turning red," I said.

"I-" he stammered.

None of the girls liked him and he didn't have any alpha qualities that made guys popular in school or in real life. But Paul had nice blue eyes and long lashes. A kind and sensitive face. The face of a poet.

Not like the face of a jock like Chad Ascott.

"So tomorrow, there is a test," Paul said, breaking the awkward silence. "I think you should do well. If you study-"

Paul flipped his well-worn green Algebra textbook open. "Doing proportions is something that you can apply to real life. Say for instance you're selling wrists bands at the flea market. Say you sold five wrist bands for a twenty dollar profit. If you have twenty wrist bands how many can you sell? You have to think of it that way. Make it relatable."

He took out a piece of scratch paper and began scrawling out the math problem. "5 over twenty is to 10 over X. What is X?"

I heard his voice but no longer paid him any attention.

Chad Ascott walked by the library and saw me through the glass. We locked eyes and he smiled. Then went off with his "boys."

Just one glance set my heart thumping like a drumbeat.

Guys like Paul would yell and scream and pout and then scream for attention from girls that they would never get.

Chad Ascott didn't have to do a damn thing but lock his eyes with a girl.

"Are you listening?" Paul asked

"What? I'm sorry, yeah."

Paul paused for a beat. "This is going to be our last session together," he suddenly looked nervous. "I wanted to give you this."

He passed me a note. Handwritten with love hearts all over it. He got up abruptly and walked off. I stared down at the note.

A love letter no doubt. But not from the boy I wanted it to be from.

Paul stepped outside. He looked back at me, pondered his romantic fate, then hurried to class.

CHAPTER THREE

"Well, this is a change," Paul laughed as I dipped my foot into the bay waters.

"How do you mean?"

"I remember back in high school you were always Miss Fashion. Not that you don't look good now. But-" he looked down on my shoe.

"I'm glad one of us can laugh about it," I said in a teasing tone.

"You look the same," he said. "And I mean that as a compliment."

"Thanks."

I lifted the shoe up and didn't see a trace of the crap.

"How long has it been since we've seen each other?"

"Ten years. Ten years exactly. There is the reunion tonight. How ironic. You going?"

"Yeah, that's what I'm in town for. Really easy to get these things together with Facebook and all."

He looked me up and down again.

"You checking me out?"

"You're hair is different but you look the same," then he looked down like he used to as a shy thirteen year old boy. "I used to have a crush on you."

"I remember," I said. "I remember when you gave me that love letter after tutoring me in Algebra."

"Oh God," he said. "I can't believe you remember that. The things we do when we're young."

"No, it was cute," I said.

"Didn't get me anywhere. I grew up and learned my lesson."

The way he said it made me hurt for him. I didn't realize how much it must have hurt him to have unrequited love.

"No," I said. "It was cute. It mattered."

"Really?"

He looked at me with a spark in his eyes then seemed to change his mind about getting into a deep in the weeds conversation.

"I learned that women really don't care about that stuff. They only care about money. Or looks. Not including you in that condemnation. Just that after high school that is what I encountered in the outside world."

He laughed and shook his head. "I'd actually give anything to be that little boy again. You know. To have an innocent crush on a beautiful girl."

I stared into his eyes. I couldn't help it. He looked handsome. Damn handsome. I had to tell him.

"I kept that note," I said.

"What?"

"That love letter you gave me. I still have it."

CHAPTER FOUR

I never told anyone about that note. I read it and re-read it.

He gushed about his love for me. How much he cherished our time together in the tutoring sessions.

At the end of the note, he declared his desire to have the last dance with me at the upcoming junior high ball.

I have to admit, I didn't know how to respond. I didn't want to hurt him yet and I didn't want to dance with him.

What if Chad saw us together?

I entered the ball with four of my girlfriends, Tiffany Marie leading the way. I saw Paul helping with the decorations then skulking near the wall. I avoided any eye contact with him.

"Why don't you ask Paul to dance?" Tiffany Marie asked sarcastically. The whole group of girls laughed as we looked over and saw him adjust his black-rimmed glasses.

I hoped he didn't hear her.

Nobody danced at eight grade "dances." People just milled around listening to the music of the day. We drank punch and ate cookies.

Our chaperones were the teachers and student aides. Two of the teachers, Mr. and Mrs. Barrington took to the dance floor and began dancing to a hip hop beat. The kids hooted and hollered. They implored other students to come in and dance but no one did.

The girls were content to whisper and steal glances from the boys they had crushes on. The boys struck poses. They would all would rather be home nursing the latest video game on their X-Box.

Out of the corner of my eye, I saw Paul. He alternated between fixing a wall decoration that said "Welcome!" and sitting in a corner chair.

He looked over at me and I quickly turned my head.

I didn't want to establish eye contact. But maybe by doing that I already hurt him.

"Why y'all ain't dancing?!" the DJ bellowed out from behind the turntable.

But he knew the answer to the question. No one wants to dance to the fast music.

They were all waiting for the slow song.

The mating dance of eye contact, sly smiles and love notes would all culminate in this song. The school year was about to end. All of the hopes, dreams and romantic wishes were leading up to who you were dancing with when that soft ballad came on.

Looking back, I realized how much of it resembled real life in a way. Some of us would find someone to pair off with. Then the song would end and we'd go our separate ways. Others would slink away and lean against the wall, pretending to enjoy themselves in the happiness of others. Some of the girls would escape to the bathroom to cry their eyes out when the boy they wanted so bad asked someone else and not them.

School dances could be cruel.

The song came on. A piano ballad from the Jets called "Make it Real". A mournful song of unrequited love.

I could feel Paul walking toward me. Looking across, I established eye contact for the first time. I didn't know what to say. I would just go with it. To see where it led.

Until Chad Ascott stepped in front of me.

"Hey," he said.

"Hey."

"Let's dance."

"Okay."

I felt the envious eyes of every girl on me. I placed my hands on his already broad shoulders and we swayed softly to the music.

"My name is Chad," he said.

"I know."

We danced in silence for a minute, then I rested my head against his chest. A dream come true. We swayed around and I saw Paul heading toward the exit.

His head bowed.

Was he crying?

I didn't care.

I had Chad.

CHAPTER FIVE

Paul and I ended up at the mini-mall which the trail led straight into. He chained up Chubbs outside the pizza joint now called *Al's* but back when we were teens it was called *Tony's*.

If you had no where else to go, you would go to Tony's. Homemade cheese slices with grilled onions.

"We used to go here for church socials, remember?"

"Yep," I said. "And everything else. Remember they had the Pac Man machine on the side?"

"Pac Man and Galaxian," he said.

We sat down and ordered a small cheese pizza.

"So much for my morning run," I said.

"Didn't look like you got very far," he laughed. "I mean, you weren't sweating when I caught up to you."

"Ugh," I said. "Does it still smell?"

"No," he said. "How do you like teaching?"

"It has its moments," I said. "But it is rewarding. I get to know the kids. I feel like it has meaning."

"That's the important part," he said. "I mean our generation is all about ambition. There really is no meaning. Really refreshing to hear you like what you do."

I noticed him looking at my ring finger.

"No, I'm not married," I waved my hand at him.

"Mind reader," he laughed. "Neither am I."

"Had a few near misses."

"I've dodged a few bullets myself."

"I'm sure you've broken quite a few hearts," I said.

"He sure has," came a sing-song voice from behind me.

Paul got up and I watched as he hugged a tall blonde woman. When I say tall, I mean tall, like six feet in her heels. Lean, tanned and just plain stunning.

I felt three feet tall in my sweat pants and no make-up look.

"This is Amber," he said.

"Hi," I said offering my hand.

She shook it with limp enthusiasm as my heart broke in two.

CHAPTER SIX

I dated Chad Ascott all through high school.

I had looked forward to senior prom night for four years. On the scale of life events for a teenager it outranked the eighth grade ball by leaps and bounds. The senior prom was *the* night. And that slow dance was *the* dance.

So when the soft ballad started to play, I desperately looked for Chad.

I looked everywhere on the dance floor.

The music didn't stop!

I opened the side door and went into the hallway. Then, in the furthest corner I saw him.

Making out with Tiffany Marie.

"You creep!" I cried out.

He turned around and smiled that smile of his. "I'm sorry," he said. "It's only a kiss."

Tiffany Marie could only look at her feet in embarrassment.

"I don't friggin' believe this," I said as I stormed back into the hall.

I had no idea where to go. The song played on. I didn't care. I wanted to leave.

"Jennifer," he called out. "Just wait."

Chad caught up to me and spun me around before I reached the opposite door.

"Don't touch me," I said.

"It was only a kiss," Chad said. "Come on. Have this dance with me. We've been waiting for this."

"You get the award for the lamest man in history. In history!"

I turned back around and he ran in front of me, blocking my way.

"Jennifer, please."

"Get away!" I pushed him and he looked pissed.

"Whatever bitch," he said.

"Who are you calling bitch, *bitch*?" Paul said.

"Are you friggin' kidding me?" Chad said, incredulous that Paul stepped to him. He pointed his finger in Paul's chest. "What are you going to do about it, you skinny twerp?"

"Touch her again-"

"And?

"And you'll see-"

Chad pushed Paul to the ground hard. Paul bolted up and pushed him back. Chad hauled off and swung with a big right. Paul leaned back but the punch still grazed his nose.

He sniffed and shrugged it off like a prize fighter.

"Want some more?" Chad asked, his quivering voice betraying his bravado.

Paul ran in and tackled his football playing nemesis. The two rolled around on the ground as Paul's arms snaked around Chad's neck.

And he put the jock to sleep just as Principal Slager arrived.

"Did you kill him?" he asked.

"Sleeper hold," Paul said. "He'll wake up in a minute."

The principal leaned down and checked Chad's pulse just in case.

"Are you all right?" Paul asked me, rubbing his bloodied nose.

I could only nod my head.

"I'll drive you home," he said, grabbing my hand as he ran toward his car.

"Demarest!" the principal cried out."Demarest get back here."

"Where'd you learn to fight like that?" I asked as we reached his car.

"I took a martial arts class," he said. "Brazilian jiu jitsu. I practiced the same move over and over again. Just in case. I guess it worked."

"I hope Chad is all right," I said.

Then I saw his entire body just deflate as he held the door open for me.

CHAPTER SEVEN

I came casually dressed to the reunion with Tiffany Marie. Yes, that Tiffany Marie.

She connected on Facebook with me a few years back and she apologized.

I didn't condemn her. We were young. Very young.

She married an Army captain but then divorced. She referred to her husband as "that hairy bastard" and "that punk ass" which I found amusing. She had a son, Jake, who wound up in my first grade class. A great kid and we hit it off.

Tiffany Marie worked in the Financial District in San Francisco. She hated her boss and the people she worked with but remained adamant about becoming a dancer "one day" and taught Jazzercise on the weekends.

"You should come by," she said. "I'll get you back in shape."

"Thanks," I said, wondering why my daily forty-minute jogs didn't register on my figure. "You'll never believe who I ran into today. Paul Demarest. Do you remember him?"

"Your knight in shining armor." she laughed.

"You remember that?" I laughed.

"How is he?"

"Girl," I whispered. "Totally different. I mean a totally changed man. A hunk."

"Really?"

"He has a girlfriend though so that really killed it."

"She's not my girlfriend," his voice boomed behind me.

Oops. I looked back at him then at Tiffany Marie. How long had he been there?

Judging from her facial expression he had been there the whole time.

"Hi Paul," Tiffany Marie said. "I've heard a lot about you."

"All good, I hear."

"Of course," she said. "Well, I'll leave you two alone."

And with that Tiffany Marie skedaddled out of the way.

As the DJ began to played a slow song that sounded just a bit too familiar.

"Do you remember this song?" Paul asked. "The Jets. Make It Real. This song played during our eighth grade dance. I was going to ask you to dance before a certain someone interrupted me."

"Oh," I said.

"May I have this dance? Because I don't see that certain someone around anymore."

"Of course," I said.

We danced through the song. I placed my head on his chest as I listened to the bittersweet ballad. Mark and Angie danced next to us. They were high school sweethearts that married immediately after graduating.

We could have been like them. If I only had said 'yes' to Paul. Why didn't I?

"*Give me one more chance to make it real,*" the song went on.

Can I really have that chance?

CHAPTER EIGHT

Paul drove me home in silence that prom night. My words had hurt him. My own heart had been crushed and Paul's feelings had been the furthest thing from my mind. I only thought of Chad. Where I went wrong with him. And how my best friend Tiffany Marie could betray me.

I always thought I was prettier than her.

I looked over at Paul and wished I could have his love for me transported into Chad's body. That would be the perfect boyfriend.

Because I saw something in Chad's smile that night. I saw that dimpled smirk for what it was when I confronted him. Chad's eyes didn't change at all but the corners of his mouth went up as if they were being pulled by puppet strings.

A young man with a fake smile.

That made him dangerous.

And that is what drew me to him.

But now it repulsed me.

"I would never hurt you like that," Paul said.

I tried to answer him but fought back tears instead. "Thanks."

"I mean, if we could you know, maybe go out sometime."

Paul pulled up in front of my house.

"Paul, I-"

He looked lost in his own world as he looked up at my home.

"I used to walk by your house on the way to school. I used to time your route because I knew the exact time you would leave the house. But then Chad started picking you up in freshman year. And I stopped passing by your house. I would take the long way. I'd go around. I couldn't bear to see you with him."

"I'm sorry."

"No need to apologize. You have free will. We can't control who we are attracted to."

I just nodded my head.

"But maybe, just maybe, if we could spend time together."

I knew what he would say next. I really didn't know how to let him down gently.

"I'd always treat you nice. I would never kiss another girl. Wouldn't need to-" he laughed.

I liked his laugh. I liked him. Just not in that way. "You're a really sweet guy, Paul."

"But-"

"But," I said. "I just don't feel it for you. Do you know what I mean-"

"Say no more," he said.

"I don't want us to be enemies at all."

"Of course not."

"I mean, I don't want you to be all weird around me at school."

"I'm always weird. I can't help it. Just like the way I can't help falling in love with you. But that's life. We always want the things we can't have,right? I remember Pastor Parker saying that once. I have loved you from afar since the moment I saw you. Since what? Seventh grade when you moved out here?"

"That's a long time to love someone, Paul."

"You're the most beautiful woman in history."

I wanted to laugh but stopped myself when I saw the tears well up in his eyes.

He got out and opened the door for me. I stepped out.

"Good bye, Jennifer," he said.

"Good bye."

I gave him a limp hug and he returned the gesture.

I don't remember seeing him much the remaining part of the year. He didn't show up at any of the senior parties. He sort of faded out. I looked for him on occasion during school lunch periods but never saw him.

I never forgot that look he gave me when he opened the door for me.

I never had a man look at me the same way ever since. Love. Longing. Passion. Kindness.

Yet, I went to sleep that night thinking of Chad.

CHAPTER NINE

Tiffany Marie decided to drive over for a night cap at McGee's, the local Irish pub. Paul offered to take me home.

I thought about the last time he drove me home on that fateful night ten years ago.

"Tiffany hasn't changed much," Paul said.

He drove an Escalade which looked brand new. I didn't ask what he did for a living but he had a moneyed air about him.

"Oh God," I said. "Some people, yeah they don't change. They just get worse."

I referred to the fact that Tiffany asked every man at the party about their relationship status. On the prowl for her next meal ticket, I thought to myself.

"It was good to see some of the old faces. I mean, I wasn't that popular in high school. Hated it actually. But people change. Nice to see how people turned out."

"Yeah," I said, showing him that I can hold my own in any conversation.

"Facebook is the equalizer, I guess. You can see how people's lives turned out."

"I didn't realize you became so-" I didn't really want to say it without sounding like a gold digger.

"Successful?" he asked. "I just got into software. It was a one shot deal. I developed an app and it took off and sold like crazy. That was it. Pure luck."

"But you still had to work hard."

He just shook his head. "Everything is just luck. People flatter themselves with hard work. I know when we were kids we were taught that so and so is blessed and so and so is blessed. Well, if there is blessing that implies that there is a curse."

"I don't think like that."

"I do. Because it's true. I was blessed in business. Cursed in love."

"But look at you. You're like a total stud now."

"Deep down I'm still the nerd that writes girls love letters."

"Oh, so there was more than one?"

"Ha, ha," he said. "You think you were the only one."

"Not anymore apparently. What's her name, April?"

"She's not my girlfriend. Just a friend. Girl I used to work with."

"So it's not serious?"

"A serious friendship, sure," he laughed. "She's not my type."

"Turn left here," I said. I felt like driving in circles just to keep the conversation going.

"Do you still go to church?" he asked.

"I still go every now and then. When I was young I just found the teachings to be stultifying. Now that I'm older I cherish the time I had there. I looked to God in my hours of need. Which is about every day dealing with some of those kids. But I wish I had spent more time in church, not in the pew but more time, I don't know, taking it seriously. I miss, you know, starting a family and having a traditional, you know...Husband, kids, picket fence and a dog."

"As long as you have plenty of Mutt Mitts."

"Right," I said. "Do you still go?"

"I stopped going after you rejected me."

"Are you serious?"

"Yes," he said. "No, I'm joking..Actually, I stopped going after my parents split up. I realized that family life wasn't really like what the people in the church portrayed. People aren't always happy, warm and friendly in real life. I had an uncle commit suicide. I used to think he was Superman. Vietnam war vet. Green Beret. My aunt left him and he became a drunk then shot himself."

"I'm sorry."

"Then I had a cousin die of a drug overdose. They raised her in church, you know, she sang all the hymns, said the right things and no one thought she was in any kind of trouble. Things, I don't know, don't always work out they're taught in church, you know? I mean sometimes you can do everything by the Christian book and things turn out bad."

"This is my stop here," I said. "The one with the brick foundation."

"Hey," he said. "You've done all right by yourself."

"I try."

"Remember the last time I drove you home. It was the last time we spoke."

"I remember."

"Really?"

"Yes, of course."

"All of this time I thought I was one of those people that isn't remembered. One of those people that everyone forgets about over time. I was such a dork."

"I remembered you. I remembered the way you spoke about how pretty you thought I was. I hope that doesn't embarrass you. Such passion. I didn't realize it at the time, you know. We just don't know what is puppy love and what is real and what really matters."

"I pedestalized true love too much. Thought there was the special one. Thought you were it. I was a silly kid."

"Its what you felt," I said. "You should never lose that. Never lose that passion."

"It fades over time. Your heart becomes calloused."

"That's too bad."

I wish I had something more eloquent to say. I wanted that same passion back. I would have given anything for this man with his blue-purple colored eyes to look deep into my soul and tell me that he had undying love for me. Like a school boy.

"I remember I had this whole speech laid out for you that night. How I would declare my love for you and you would love me and kiss me forever. It was all so-"

I reached over and kissed him. Kissed him like I had never kissed anyone before in my life.

CHAPTER TEN

We laid in bed. I had my head on his chest just like it was when we danced only hours earlier.

"This isn't a one night stand," he said.

"I know."

I traced my finger across his chest.

"I didn't treat you right," I said. "I didn't see you for what you were to become. Even so, that didn't matter. It is who you are that counts. Not what."

"We were young," he said. "People only want the things they can't have. Like Chad Ascott."

"Chad Ascott. Jesus."

"They say high school is supposed to be the best years of your life," he said. "I don't know about that. You wait and wait for your life to start, you know. Work takes out whole chunks of your life and you wonder when the good stuff starts, or has it already been and gone, I don't know."

"I wished things could have been different for us. Like maybe we could have been like Angie and what's his name?"

"High school sweethearts," he said. "That's nice. But we ended up together. Here. Now."

"Yes," I said.

We kissed. Again and again.

I looked into his eyes. He did change. He had that look of a marathon runner who had begun to wonder if the prize is worth the race.

"What did your parents say to you when they divorced?"

"What everyone else says. That they loved me and nothing that happens will change that."

"Well, whatever happens between us now, I just want to let you know that I love you. Nothing will ever change that."

He kissed me. But in his eyes I saw something different. A sort of lost innocence that we can't really can't back. Reflections of all the women that have hurt him over the years.

And he saw the ghosts of all of the men I had been with.

I kissed him anyway. Then we hugged and I saw my reflection in the glass window.

I hoped to see the same hopeful schoolgirl. Instead I saw a scared woman.

Love is so hard. Twelve. Eighteen or Twenty-eight.

The things we do to each other.

I kissed him again.

And hoped.

ANNALEISE

Annaleise rolled over in her cotton sheets and stared out the window at the sun beaming through the ragged curtains of her bedroom. The light from the morning lit up the interior of her modest room. The cock crowed as she stirred and stepped from the comfort of the warm bed. As her delicate toes touched the floor she winced at the feel of the cool floorboards beneath her feet. She mentally prepared herself for another typical day in the remote Amish community where she was raised. She sat on the edge of her bed and began braiding her long, golden locks. Her hair had never been cut. Once finished she tied a tiny, white bow at the end. Standing up, her hair extended all the way down to her upper thighs.

From the homely bedside table, she grabbed her prayer cap, the white cap made of organza and stiff with starch that she must wear in public. She slipped it over her long, golden braid and stood, making her way over to the wardrobe, barefoot. The floorboards creaked beneath her slender frame. The house in which she lived was in need of much repair, but it was home.

Her dress was bound by the Amish community to which she belonged. She pulled out the calf-length, gray dress, and her white apron to accompany it. She looked the outfit up and down, sighing at the restrictions she had to abide by. Just a little color or a little lace would make it so much more tolerable, but alas it was forbidden.

She slipped the dress over her head, atop the white, cotton undergarments she wore beneath. Her slender arms penetrated the long sleeves at the ends and her delicate fingers stretched out toward the floor. Her blue eyes reflected in the full-length mirror that stood opposite. They ran over her entire frame, assessing the modesty of her attire. Her smooth legs peeked out the bottom of the gown. Her hands just protruded from the sleeves. How she longed for something different. To have somewhat more choice when it came to the little things. But living here her options were overly restricted. With a sigh, she turned away from her dull reflection.

Her stomach growled lightly, alerting her that breakfast time was upon her. Before leaving, she quickly raced to the window and opened it wide, allowing the cool morning air to hit her face. It almost stung as the contrasting wind nipped at her warm skin. She turned on her heels and made her way to the exit of her humble sanctuary, ready to start the day ahead.

Before opening the door she took a deep breath, hearing the faint clip-clop of hooves outside. She felt a tear well up in the corner of her eye, but she willed it to stop. No matter how much she tried, Annaleise was overwhelmed with pain with any reminder of her parent's accident. No day since their passing had her parent's death become any easier for Annaleise. Each day she was reminded of the terrible accident they had undertaken. As soon as she set eyes on the cart outside, laying rusted and disheveled. Unused for a year. A constant visual scar, sitting in their front yard. Although she knew that her brother, Jacob, shared her pain she would not dare discuss with him.

He had been walking down the street when it occurred. On his way back from the cornfields down the road from their home. Their mother and father waved as they passed, smiling at him. The next thing Jacob knew, he was watching their cart overturn as the horses bucked and bolted, leaving the two bodies trapped beneath the wreckage. Around him, people screamed at the sight, but all he could do was rush over to find his parents laying lifeless in the middle of the dirt road.

Annaleise was distraught. She cried for weeks. She took to her room and moped. No one could comfort her. Since then the community had done their best to assist the two orphaned children. They stayed in the family home, but here they could barely make ends meet. Her job as a milkmaid at the dairy farm and his as an apprentice blacksmith left them living pay day to pay day. They relied on handouts from neighbors and friends to feed themselves. Still, Annaleise and

Jacob vowed to take care of themselves, and that was just what they did. Regardless of if it was against the rules.

One evening, months after the accident, Jacob had an idea. He weighed it up in his mind over and over. He had promised Annaleise the day of their parents passing that he would always take care of her. That was just what he intended to do. But not if it meant risking her safety or standing within the community. Finally, he decided that there was no other option for them. The need for financial stability was too great.

"Come out with me tonight," he had asked, his voice trembling with what she felt to be nerves, excitement or worry, she could not distinguish.

"To where?" she had asked, but he would not answer. Annaleise was wary at first of her brother's sudden plan. Still, she trusted him and so she followed, through the woods and to the city on the other side.

"Where are we going, Jacob?" she asked on their journey. He turned and held out his hand, signaling her to stop in her tracks. He opened the knapsack he had been holding tightly to his chest since they had left the community. Inside was a range of colorful clothing, the likes of which Annaleise had never seen.

"I am taking you to the city," he explained, pulling out a pale pink fitted dress and white heels for his sister. She stared in awe at the strange fabric garments handed to her.

"You need to wear these, otherwise they will know we are not from there," he explained. Entering a modern city in their modest attire would surely give them away as patrons of the well-known Amish district just miles away. Jacob had experienced this prejudice first hand after all.

"I will stand over there. Let me know when you have changed. You can put your clothes in this bag," he gestured to the bag from which he had pulled the new outfit. Then he turned and walked out of sight, giving his sister the privacy to change.

She untied her apron and dropped her dress to the forest floor. She folded them and placed them in the knapsack Jacob had provided. She shivered in the cold night air. Picking up the new dress she pulled it gingerly over her head. It was so tight and firm around her body. She looked down at herself in the odd creation. Quickly she slipped the heels on her feet and called out,

"I think I am ready Jacob!" moments later he emerged from the shadows. He paused, taken aback by his sister's speedy transformation. He took her hand and kicked the knapsack into a large bush beside them.

"Time to go then," he whispered and they were off again through the trees.

When they came out on the other side of the vast wood, Annaleise stopped in awe. The lights glistened in the distance as they looked over the high-rise jungle. Jacob had been lucky enough to experience life on the other side. This is where he had been during Rumspringa, but his freedom was short-lived. He promptly returned to the community, overwhelmed by the progression he experienced.

Annaleise had not had that luxury. This was her first time in the city, even seeing it from a distance.

"Why are you bringing me here?" she mumbled. Jacob's expression became serious.

"We need money, Annaleise. I did not want to worry you with such matters but since our parents passing we have been struggling... more than you know." she had no idea what this had to do with going to the city.

"We can get jobs here. Second jobs, at night. It has been so hard for us Annaliese and I need your help. Please," he begged. But she would do anything for her brother. She took his hand once more and squeezed it kindly.

"Then let's go," she said, excitedly.

Months later and they had been working at the diner quite regularly, almost every night. Annaleise darted around in her short, yellow waitressing uniform, serving tables left and right. After her first day, she was amazed at how much money she had made, and just in tips. In the kitchen her brother worked hastily, cleaning dish after dish and piles of cutlery. But neither of them minded the hard work, especially Annaleise. She was happy to just be out in the real world.

"Order up!" the chef boomed from the service window. He rang the bell relentlessly to alert her of food being ready to pick up. She scooted over and took it to her waiting customers. Now she had everything down to a fine art.

The sneaking around was getting quite cumbersome, however. Her heart raced each night her and Jacob ventured out, against the communities wishes. That night when she got home she collapsed on the bed and stared up at the ceiling. Exhausted, she wished her life was more simple. Leading her dual existence was taking its toll on her. She was plagued with a lack of sleep and a crippling anxiety. Tossing and turning during her few hours sleep each night. Alas, she had no other choice, for now anyway. She felt a huge debt weighing on her, for her brother. He had taken care of Annaleise since their parent's sudden demise. No matter how much she wished she could leave, it was not an option.

One morning as she was walking down the street, Annaleise was greeted by an unexpected face.

"Annaleise!" a man's voice boomed from behind her. She turned quickly on her heel to see an old friend, one whom she thought had left for good years earlier.

"Jebidiah?" she said, stunned. Her grocery basket fell to the ground with a thud as she ran toward him and wrapped her arms around his broad shoulders. He picked her up around the waist and they held their embrace for several seconds. Even though it had been so long since their last encounter, neither failed to recognize the other.

He dropped her back to the ground and she stepped back slightly to take in the sight of her long lost friend. His hair was styled just as it always had been. His dark brown locks were cut short, a few inches from his scalp. It hung in waves around his face. His skin was tanned and contrasted perfectly with his strong, masculine jawline and muscular figure. His chin was littered with stubble, giving his face a slight shadowing.

Their last meeting had not been so joyous. Jebidiah had been leaving for Rumspringa with her brother Jacob. The three children had grown up as close as they could be, spending endless hours together playing in the cornfields and chasing each other through the streets. Since the age of five, Annaleise and Jebidiah had known each other. She saw him as one of her closest friends. Or at least she had before he disappeared.

It had been a cold night, pelting down with rain. They stood there, facing each other. Annaleise had been fifteen, Jebidiah sixteen. Not a word was spoken for several minutes between them. Too young to realize the deep feelings that connected them, Jebidiah left with Jacob, to experience the modern world with the rest of the community boys coming of age that year. Annaleise had waited for him. She waited up at night and watched for him during the day. But he did not return.

Jacob came back weeks later with a few of the neighborhood boys, but Jebidiah was not among them.

Her brother had rested his hand on her shoulder as tears rolled down her face, tears for the loss of her best friend.

"He said to tell you he will see you again. He promised." at the time Annaleise had not believed him. She had thought her brother was trying desperately to bring her out of her deepening hole of overwhelming sadness. But with Jebidiah standing before her, Jacob's words echoed in the midst of her thoughts.

'He promised.'

She had given up hope of seeing him again, yet here he stood, in the flesh.

Jebidiah was speechless. He had returned to the community after years. It seemed that no matter how much the modern world drew him, his love for Annaleise was stronger. From the day he had left, he did not stop thinking about her, not for a moment. It had been fun and he savored the new experiences put forth by his peers in the city, but no one could replace her. That was what influenced him to return. There was nothing more he could gain from the city, he was looking to start a family. Jebidiah could not consider anyone else he would rather make a life with than her.

"I hope Jacob gave you my message all those years ago," he said, smiling down at her from above.

"He did," she replied, mirroring the beam that had taken over Jebidiah's face. Any onlooker could tell that these two were much more than just friends, even if they had not yet admitted it to themselves. They still grasped the hands of each other as they chatted for a few minutes about shared memories from the past.

Jebidiah bent down and picked up the discarded basket of groceries Annaleise had dropped in her shock at his appearance.

"Let's go for a walk, I need to catch up with you. So much has happened in the last few years I am sure," he laughed. As they strolled along they spoke at length about their experiences. Everything Jebidiah said about his time away absolutely intrigued her. She desperately wished that she could share in this modern world, if only for a day. Working was all she had ever had the chance to do when her and Jacob managed to escape for their night shifts.

"So, what about your life, Annaleise?" he questioned. After a moment of thought, he saw her face drop. The only significant thing she could think of to tell him was of her parent's sudden demise the previous fall. She took a deep breath and prepared herself for the retelling of the most painful memory she possessed.

"Actually, there was an accident last year," she began. Jebidiah's permanent grin faded almost immediately.

"My parents cart overturned. It was terrifying but the worst was that they did not make it." Jebidiah could not find the words to express his condolences. After a few moments to comprehend the brief and saddening story he mustered,

"I am so sorry, Annaleise."

As always, her first thought was to change the subject, and so she did. Long ago she had decided that her parents would not have wanted her to mourn, but cherish the life that she had. That was exactly what she intended to do. The sadness they had been wallowing in for that brief moment evaporated quickly as they moved on to more trivial and light-hearted news from their vast time apart.

Jebidiah walked her all the way back to her door. He handed back the basket as she stepped through the threshold of the dark, polished doorway.

"Well, I am sure we will see each other again soon," he said as he turned to leave.

"You will," she smiled and with that the door clicked shut behind her.

As the following months flew by, Annaleise found herself spending more and more of her limited free time with her long lost friend. Jebidiah found comfort in their closeness. Since moving back, he had faced endless scrutiny from the older members of the place he called home. They frowned upon him for his rash decision to leave, now that he had returned. He had known upon his abrupt return to his family that not everyone would be so welcoming. But no one else mattered as long as Annaleise was by his side.

She found comfort in his company too. She was intrigued by his endless stories of the new technologies and strange architecture he had encountered in his years away. Unlike her peers, Annaleise held nothing against him for leaving, if anything she wished that she could do the same.

The two companions spent their time just as they did, years earlier. Exploring the now familiar woods. Chasing each other through the cornfields. Collapsing with laughter on the dirt floor of the outdoors. They savored each moment they spent in each others company. To Annaleise, no one could compare to Jebidiah.

One sunny afternoon, they fell into each other's arms in the dewy grass of the outskirts of the boundary. Their laughter subsided and Annaleise looked up at Jebidiah, beaming down at her. She knew that there was something deeper. This was not just another friendship, he meant so much more. Every second without him left her feeling cold and empty. Every second without her made him feel as if he was completely alone.

"Do you think you will stay here this time?" Annaleise asked. She hoped that his answer reflected the way that she felt. But alas, he uttered the answer she did not want to hear.

"No. I think that now I have experienced what is out there, lived my life outside the confines of the community, I don't want to leave again." her heart dropped. There was nothing in the world she wished for more than to go, but a life without Jebidiah seemed just as empty.

It was his strength that encouraged her to plan her escape, to a new life in the modern world. Deep in her heart she knew that it was unlikely Jebidiah would come with her. After all, he had returned not weeks ago, but she had to follow her dreams. She had but one life, and she intended to live it. As much as she wanted to share with him her wishes, she knew this was one secret she must keep to herself.

Jebidiah walked her home again that day, as he often did of late. The sun was setting over the sovereign hills as they strolled past people and places on the way home. She took in the sights, for in a few weeks they would be gone forever. There was no doubt she would miss this place, but most of all she would miss him. She cherished the time they had together, though short lived.

They arrived at her home. Before she opened the door, Jebidiah grasped her wrist tightly. Her skin broke out in goosebumps all over in response to his flesh against hers. Her heart raced within her chest cavity. Cheeks began to glow red as the blood from her pounding heart rushed to her face. She hoped that Jebidiah did not see the intense reaction she gave from his touch.

"Do you have plans for tomorrow?" he questioned. His expression was serious all of a sudden.

"No," Annaleise responded. Where was he going with this?

"I see, well goodnight then," he said with a grin. How strange. With that Jebidiah let go of her arm and placed his hands into his pockets.

"Goodbye," she called to him as he strolled slowly away, toward his family home at the end of the road.

As she closed the door behind her Annaleise leaned her back against the rough wood and closed her eyes. The overwhelming sensation of lust she felt for Jebidiah was quickly blooming into a raging passion. Love. Little did she know that he felt it too. From the top of her head to the far tips of her toes her entire being was filled with admiration and desire for him. How would she tell him that she was going to leave the town? Start a new life in the place that he had run from.

She already had a plan in place. Two weeks from now she would be living amongst the modern world. Jacob had not been pleased, but he knew that he could not stop his sister from following her dreams. He had the opportunity, so there was no way that he could deny her that right, regardless of the community law.

"Are you sure you will be OK on your own?" Jacob could not hide the worried tone of his voice. Not even he could brave the new world, how could his little sister live there alone?

"I will, please do not worry about me, Jacob," then she explained her plan.

In the dead of night, while the town slept, she would sneak silently through the streets. Toward the wood. The path that they had traveled hundreds of times before would lead her to her new existence. She could not leave during the day, for fear of what scrutiny she may face from the others in the town. Women rarely left and were never welcomed home. It was best for her to just disappear.

"But you have never been that way alone." he said, his voice still trembling with fear for Annaleise.

"I have mapped out our way. The last few weeks I have made a note of each landmark along the path. Each time I feel as if my feet lead me more and more. I step without hesitation." slowly she had memorized the way. Every rock and tree, branch and shrub. The dirt clearings and the overgrown mangling of tangled weeds, she was confident in her navigational ability. Even if Jacob was not so.

"Where will you stay?" his questions kept coming. But Annaleise was not one to take her decisions lightly. To his every question, she had the perfect answer. During their time at the diner, they had made a few friends, both co-workers, and customers. Annaleise had organized a room in a modest apartment with Katie, a fellow waitress at a neighboring restaurant. For only a small portion of her minimum wage, she had a place to her her own.

Several hours later, Annaleise had assured her brother that she could fend for herself. If she ever needed him, he would be there for her too.

Jacob took her hand and looked at her, eyes full of sadness.

"I will always be here for you, sister," a single tear rolled down his cheek, winding its way through the stubble on his strong chin. Annaleise was taken aback, she had not seen her brother so emotional since their parents passing. She whispered the only words that came to mind in response to his heartfelt confession.

"I know," tears now flowed freely down their faces. They sat in silence as Jacob took in the news she had revealed to him. The plan she had derived. How much he would miss her.

The hardest part was over. Annaleise had dreaded telling her brother about her escape. Now she felt free, with his blessing she could leave without hesitation. She slept that night, soundly for the first time in many moons. Dreaming of the future adventures she would have in the big city.

The next morning Jebidiah was at her door before either of the siblings had risen. She heard the light tapping from her bedroom and quickly dressed to see who was so desperate to see them this day. She raced down the creaking steps and to the front door. Opening it widely she was ecstatic to see Jebidiah standing there with a bouquet of red roses. Their scent was swept immediately into her nostrils and she closed her eyes as the aroma intoxicated her.

"Good morning, Annaleise," Jebidiah greeted her, placing the stunning bunch into her hands.

"Hello," she replied, staring at the gift he had brought for her. Something was different about him this morning. She could not pick it but his smile was strange somehow, brighter than she had seen before. His eyes sparkled in the morning light. Her heart skipped a beat as they paused for a moment, looking deeply into each other's eyes.

"I have a day planned for us," he said excitedly. Before she had time to properly lace up her boots, Jebidiah took her hand and whisked her away from her home. They walked together toward the vast cornfields at the end of the street. Waving at their fellow community members as they passed, Jebidiah led Annaleise through the tall corn stalks.

She had no idea what he had in store. They rushed forward in silence. Annaleise found her mind wandering as she took in the rays of sunlight winding through the stalks and leaves surrounding them. Her dress occasionally caught on rouge sticks and branches strewn throughout the fields. She stumbled a few times, but Jebidiah was there to catch her and help her find her feet once more.

Minutes passed and they finally arrived at the small clearing in the far end of the fields. Jebidiah let her hand drop and pulled a blanket from the backpack he had been lugging with them on the short journey. He laid it delicately out on the ground, straightening the edges and patting it down flat.

"Come, sit," he gestured to a soft spot on the blanket and she slowly approached, sitting down carefully, holding her dress flat against her thighs as she lowered her body to the ground. She watched on as Jebidiah began unpacking a picnic that he had prepared. She was stunned at the romantic setting that he had created for just the two of them, out of nowhere.

"I hope you're hungry," he laughed. Her eyes drifted from plate to plate, each piled high with sandwiches and cakes, fruit and salads. She could not believe what she saw before her. This was the kind of thing she had always dreamed of but had never eventuated into a reality. The sun beamed down on them as they began their conversations.

"Please," Jebidiah picked up a plate of her favorite sandwiches, fresh strawberry jam. She picked up one and took a bite. The sweetness of the jam found every corner of her tongue, leaving a lasting sensation in her mouth as she swallowed. He watched her intently, looking as if something was weighing heavily on his mind. Annaleise looked into his deep, brown eyes. She felt herself smile as she took in his handsome features, just inches from her. His short, dark hair flowed subtly in the mild breeze. Her gaze followed his masculine jawline and rugged chin, covered in light stubble.

It was at that moment Jebidiah uttered the words she had been longing for him to say for so long,

"I love you, Annaleise, I always have." she was taken aback. Of course, her heart reciprocated his feelings, but she could not bring herself to say the words back. In the back of her mind, she knew that if she revealed her love for him she must also let him in on the fact she was planning to leave. Leave him and everything else behind. Moments later she found her voice once more,

"I love you too."

They spoke for hours after Jebidiah's unexpected, but heartfelt, confession. Of life and the paths they wanted to take in the future. That was when troubles arose.

"I just want to settle down, and have a family. I love it so much here. It feels so right to be back." Jebidiah said in between bites of his rosy red apple. Annaleise froze. This was exactly the life she was running from. It was the first time that she realized that their journeys may lead them in different directions. She sat silent for a moment as he waited patiently for her to say something, anything. She took a deep breath and proceeded to reveal her underlying plan to Jebidiah. Her plan to leave and start a new life in the city he had fled from.

"I had no idea," Jebidiah gasped, in response to her and Jacob's secret second existence outside of the community. His heart dropped as she continued to explain her plans to escape and live amongst the modern world. Never had he thought coming into the fields with her that morning that she would drop this bombshell upon him. All hopes of his quiet life back at home with his childhood sweetheart were slowly evaporating before his eyes.

"When do you plan to leave?" he questioned, his heartbeat pounding in his chest. He prayed that it was not soon. That he would have time to change her mind.

"Two weeks from today," she admitted. His smile had faded, and hers with it. She had thought that the hardest conversation before her departure was over, but she had not counted on Jebidiah's romantic notions. His proposal of a simple, family life in the mundane town she had always lived. She loved him deeply, but her want for adventure was overwhelming.

With the sun beginning to lower over the tips of the corn, they decided that it was time to return. She folded the blanket as Jebidiah picked up the empty plates that surrounded them in the clearing. He took her hand and led the way back through the towering stalks. They moved at a much slower pace upon their return. Annaleise could not be sure, maybe it was due to the dimming light, but she felt as if their lagging pace was a bi-product of the conversations they had just had. Of her leaving him and the rest of her life behind.

Eventually, they reached her front door once more. She stepped up the front stair and peered down at him.

"Thank you for today, Jebidiah. I had an amazing time. I really appreciate all that you have done for me," Annaleise checked quickly for onlookers and before a word could escape his lips she kissed him tenderly on the cheek. By the time Jebidiah realized what had happened she had already stepped back inside.

He began his journey home, filled with mixed emotions from the day just passed. He desperately wanted Annaleise to stay, but he understood her position was difficult. With constant reminders daily of her parent's death, he could only imagine the heartache she must feel living here.

Two weeks later, the grandfather clock below the stairs began chiming midnight. Annaleise knew this was her chance to make her escape quietly, without fear of waking her sleeping neighborhood. She tiptoed down the stairs, their echoing creaks masked by the gongs of the great timekeeper. Her blonde locks fell over her face as she looked down toward the door, her destination on this dark winter night. She brushed them aside and kept moving. Grabbing the already assembled knapsack from its hiding spot, she slipped her pale pink coat over her slender shoulders and on the final stroke of midnight the door clicked shut behind her.

The cool wind bit at her exposed flesh as she crept through the dead of night. She knew that by leaving she was breaking her oath to the

Church, but the call of the outside world was just too great. Not even her one true love could keep her from following her dreams. A single tear rolled slowly down her pale cheek as she looked back, back at the friends and family she would no longer see. Back at Jebidiah.

Tearing her gaze away she strove forward. Her hair was now wet with sweat, despite the cold air that stung her face and pierced her lungs. She ran, as fast as she could. Each snapping twig made her heart jump. Every sound around her made her pause for a moment. A moment was all she could spare. Slowly she kept moving, through the woods, following the hidden road to freedom. As she made her way Annaleise found her mind wandering back to all of her most cherished memories with the community and everything she was giving up. The celebrations and family dinners. Just as she lost herself completely in her thoughts a sharp noise snapped her back to reality.

She looked around desperately for somewhere to hide. She could distinguish faint footsteps coming her way. Who could be out here this late, in the cold? Annaleise was convinced that she was caught. Someone had overheard her speaking of her plan to Jebidiah, or worse he had outed her himself. She threw her knapsack into a large bush to her left and jumped behind. As she crouched on the ground crazy accusations filled her head, but she kept her blue eyes focused on the clearing before her. Was it Jebidiah who let slip her secret plan, or did someone else overhear? When a shadowy figure finally caught her eye in the woods, she waited with baited breath to identify her stalker.

Branches crunched beneath his feet as the man emerged into the grassy clearing, uncloaked by the light of the moon. Annaleise's jaw dropped and her heart raced at what felt like a thousand beats a second. She no longer needed to hide, she no longer had any fear or doubt about the path that she had chosen.

"Jebidiah!" she exclaimed, sprinting as fast as her legs could carry her toward him. A smile exploded across his face as she jumped carelessly into his outstretched arms. Jebidiah wrapped his muscular arms around her. He grasped her as tight as he could, never wanting to part again. She let her body melt into his. There they stood, nestled in each other's arms for several moments before severing their sensual embrace.

"I could not let you go, Annaleise. I love you." Jebidiah confessed. She stared into his beaming blue eyes, looking down upon her. There was only one thing that she could respond.

"I love you too," she answered. Her eyes welled up with blissful tears that soon began running, one by one, down her soft cheeks. Jebidiah reached forward and wiped them away with his calloused hands. One of her arms drew back, reaching up to run her fingers through his mess of tangled hair, damp with sweat. Still stunned by his sudden appearance, she was nothing but ecstatic to see him.

At that moment, Jebidiah leaned down and kissed her soft, cherry lips for the first time, basking in the cool blanket of moonlight penetrating the canopy. Annaleise could not believe her luck as she stood in the middle of the trees, in the arms of her love. She had been sure, not hours ago, that she had lost the love of her life forever. Now, she was on her way to making a new life for herself, in a new world, with the man of her dreams.

She leaned in closer to his warm silhouette, grasping at the fabric of his coat. She savored his touch, something she thought she had lost forever in the sands of time. His hand brushed her now flushing cheeks. He traced down her neck and over her petite shoulder. Her hand found its place against his pounding chest. And hers against his.

Jebidiah brushed a lock of hair from Annaleise's ear.

"We must go now," he whispered softly to her. Stepping back from him, she nodded in agreement. She would no longer need to start her new life alone, they were together at last. He picked up her knapsack and hauled it onto his back.

"Come," he ushered Annaleise back onto her path. Toward the city for the last time. As they neared the bustling hub, she witnessed the blanket of light illuminating the town. Never had she seen something so beautiful. Never had she felt so free.

www.ingramcontent.com/pod-product-compliance
Lightning Source LLC
Chambersburg PA
CBHW022137150726

47992CB00002B/632